COMES THE STORM

BEAR WILLIS: MOUNTAIN MAN

BOOK 14

PETER ALAN TURNER

PRODUCTIONS

Published by DS Productions

ISBN: 9798859664429

CONTENTS

1

COMES THE STORM

The Ranger should have bled to death, but the gunshot wound finally clotted up, thanks to the sleeve he had torn from his shirt and wrapped tightly around the injury. Not that it mattered much, as he had bled a frightening amount of blood and was now slipping in and out of consciousness. The rain, which had been a Godsend hours earlier when the sun had nearly baked him to a crisp, now chilled him.

Still, he was a stubborn man for someone so young. It was this cantankerous nature that had gotten him through several close calls. Hopefully, it would help him survive this one. The man didn't know exactly where he was going. All he knew was that the old mountain man and his family lived in a valley in the Franklin Mountains. His mare was born there, and he hoped the mare would remember the way home. If not, he was a dead man.

"Come on, gal. You can do it." rasped the young Texas Ranger as he clung to the horse's neck. The rain lashed at the man, threatening to sweep him off the saddle and into the mud.

Bear Willis was in a restless mood. He had tried to go to sleep but finally got up and made himself a pot of coffee. He was waiting for the coffee to brew when his wife, Waity, appeared at the bedroom door, wrapped in a hand-woven blanket.

"What's the matter?" she asked.

"Don't rightly know, Love. Just restless. I guess."

"Well, that mud you call coffee won't help. Put it down and come to bed."

"In a bit," replied Bear.

Waity had returned to her bed.

"There was a time when I would have rushed into her bed," thought Bear as he sipped his coffee and stared into the fire.

Bear finished the coffee and was about to join his wife when Thor lifted his massive head and growled. His brother Odin, sleeping before the fire, groaned and shifted slightly before settling back down. Thor growled again. "Easy, boy," said Bear as he picked up his rifle.

Bear had learned long ago to trust his Irish

Wolfhounds. Thor was always the first to sense trouble, while Odin, once alerted, was the more aggressive of the two hounds.

Bear heard a horse neigh. He blew out the candle. Now fully awake, Odin joined Thor, standing at Bear's side.

"It's a mite late for visitors," Bear whispered to the hounds, "so be ready for anything."

Suddenly, Bear heard the sound of someone rapping on the door. Immediately, the Irish Wolfhounds bared their teeth. Waity, awakened by the dogs, entered the room.

"Now, who could that be?"

"I don't know, but just to be safe, take my pistol and stand behind the chair."

His wife moved quickly, "Okay, I'm ready," she whispered.

With his rifle in one hand, Bear cracked open the wooden door. With his last ounce of strength gone, the young Ranger fell into Bear's arms, nearly bowling him.

"Waity, lend a hand. It's that young Ranger, Chet Henderson!"

"Lord, it looks like he's been shot and left for dead," exclaimed Waity as she cleared off the kitchen table. "Here, lay him down. We must get him out of those wet clothes and clean the wound before he wakes up."

Bear and Waity stripped Henderson of his sodden clothes. Then Waity covered him with a wool blanket. "Watch him while I get a bowl of water and clean cloths."

"He's been shot in the left leg, just above the knee," said

Bear, "Here, let's roll him over and see if the bullet went through."

They rolled Chet onto his right side. Bear held him while Waity examined the leg.

"It didn't go through. I can feel it just under the skin. Sharpen up your knife. You'll have to cut it out."

Bear pulled his Barlow folding knife, which he used for whittling little toys for the children, and stropped it on his belt. Bear tested the blade's edge with his thumb and nodded.

"Okay, hold him steady."

Lots of men would have hesitated, but not Bear Willis. The mountain man had performed this surgery many times, including on himself. Bear knew that the only way to do it was to make a clean cut, deep enough to extract the bullet. The faster he could do this, the less likely his patient would go into shock.

The keen edge of the knife's blade sliced into the flesh. Immediately, blood welled up and began to flow down the leg. Bear wiped away the blood and probed with the tip of the knife. "I think I can pop it."

Bear pressed on both sides of the bullet and, feeling it moved, pushed harder, forcing the lead shot out of the incision.

"There we go. Now fetch the bottle of whiskey, and I'll flush out the wound."

Years ago, an old trapper told him that a wound must

be washed with whiskey. "It might be the alcohol, but whatever it is, the whiskey helps prevent infection."

At the time, Bear thought using whiskey to wash out a cut was a terrible waste of good liquor. But, over time, the practice of cleaning a wound with whiskey proved to be effective.

"Okay, Waity, stitch him up. Me hands are too big for sewing."

An hour later, Chet Henderson was tucked into a feather bed in the spare bedroom.

"I'll sit up with him," offered Waity. "You get some sleep. I have a feeling tomorrow's going to be a busy day."

The clap of thunder woke Bear up with a start. As his mind cleared, Bear remembered what happened a few hours ago. He threw off the covers and rushed barefoot into the spare room.

"Well, I see you survived the night," said Bear.

"Thanks to you and your wife," replied Chet, between spoonfuls of Waity's chicken soup.

"My leg hurts like the dickens, but I guess I'll live."

"A young, healthy man like you would need more than a bullet in the leg to bring you down." Said Waity.

"So, lad, what happened to you?"

"We were on the hunt for some outlaws when we were bushwacked by the polecats. They killed three Rangers who were with me. As I rode away, one of them shot me in the leg. I knew I was close to your ranch. So, I just let Maggie have her head and hoped she knew the way. I was about finished when I saw the light from your cabin. I might have ridden right by if it wasn't for that light."

"You're lucky, Chet. For some reason, I couldn't sleep."

"The angels were guiding you,"" said Waity. "Usually, Bear's sleeping like a log, but not last night."

"I need to send word to Captain Wallace," said Chet. "Brett Simon is on the loose."

"Simon!" Bear spat out the name like he had a bad taste in his mouth. "I thought he was still in prison."

"Broke out about two months ago. Since then, we haven't heard or seen Simon. Until last week, when he and five hombres shot up Gordon Fisher and made off with his cattle."

Bear could feel his anger rise. "The bastard, Simon, should have hung for what he did."

"Most folks would agree with you."

"Well, you're in no shape to ride, and I need to stay here with this storm. But my son, Eric, should be here soon. He can ride down to El Paso and tell Bigfoot you're safe."

Chet smiled, "I believe you're one of only a few men who can call Captain Wallace 'Bigfoot' and get away with it.""

"Ha!" chuckled Bear, "That's because I'm bigger than the Captain."

Chet smiled, "Indeed you are." Said the Ranger.

"Henderson swallowed three more spoonfuls of soup,

then leaning his head back on a pillow, said, "Thanks, Waity, but that's enough for now."

Waity put the soup bowl on a tray. "The best thing for you to do right now is sleep. Come along, Bear, and let Chet rest."

Bear wanted to ask Chet more questions. But fearing the wrath of his wife, he decided to take her advice and wait till later.

They walked out of the bedroom. Waity put the dirty dishes in the sink, then, turning to Bear, said, "Is Chet talking about Brett Simon?"

"I'm afraid so. According to Chet, he escaped prison and is up to his old tricks of rustling cattle. A few days ago, Gordon Fisher claimed Simon shot him and stole twenty head of cattle."

"If Simon is operating in the territory, then we're all in danger. Remember what he promised!"

"I do," said Bear, "But if that son of a she-devil shows his ugly mug around here, the last thing Simon will hear is me cocking my gun! I swear he'll not get the privilege of a trial."

Bear and Waity were interrupted by their daughter Rose, "Ma, the boys are picking on me!"

Waity smiled at Bear, "I wish the rain would stop so they can get outside and let off some steam."

"Yep, not to mention doing their chores," agreed Bear. "Young'uns are not meant to be cooped up inside all day."

"I'll have Rose help me bake a chocolate cake for supper."

"And I'll take Charles and Jedediah to the barn and have them clean out the stalls."

Bear was about to call his sons when the door flew open, and in rushed Sara with her two children. "Gosh, I'm sorry about the door, but the wind blew it out of my hands."

"That's alright," replied Bear as he leaned against the door and latched it shut.

"What are you and the children doing out in this storm?" asked Bear, picking up Lizzy.

"That can wait! We need to get the children out of their wet clothes before they catch their death," ordered Waity.

"Rose, take Lizzy and Elmer to your room and find them warm clothes. I'll put the kettle on and make some cocoa. Sara, take off that oilskin and sit by the fire."

"There," said Waity, handing Sara a cup of tea, "Now, what are you doing out in this weather?"

"It's the river," replied Sara, "Last night, the river flooded its banks. This morning, the water had risen within a hundred feet of the house and barn. Eric went out to check on the horses and returned to tell me that the horses had broken out of the corral and that we were in danger of being flooded. So, I took the children and ran to your cabin to warn you."

"Where's Eric now?" asked Bear.

"He said he was going to try and find the horses. But

I'm scared. You can hardly see your hand in front of your face, and the ground is just a sea of mud. If it doesn't stop raining soon, the house and barn will be washed away."

Bear pulled on his oilskin and, pulling his hat down low, said, "I'm going out to help Eric."

Waity was going to warn him to be careful, but her words were drowned out when Bear opened the door. "I ain't never seen a storm as bad as this," said Sara.

"Nor, I," agreed Waity, "I guess this must be what it was like for Noah and his family."

"Hmm, maybe we should be building an ark," said Sara.

"Or at least a raft," added Waity.

Both women laughed, neither dreaming how their lives would be threatened in the next few hours.

2

HOW HIGH'S THE WATER?

S ara was right," thought Bear, "I can barely see the barn
through the rain."

Despite the oilskin coat, Bear was soaked when he reached the barn. He removed his hat and slapped it against his leg. "Dang, this is worse than the storm of 1836, when the Yellowstone flooded the valley and wiped out the Arapaho village."

Bear shuddered as he recalled finding the village and the bodies of the dead.

Entering the barn, Bear ducked as a chicken flapping its wings flew out the door. The hen only got a few feet before splashing into a puddle. Bear watched as the wet hen ran back into the barn. The other animals in the barn were skittish, and each new clap of thunder sent them into a panic.

Bear patted his favorite mule on the head, 'It's all right, Sally. This storm would last forever. Let's feed you and then take a ride."

Of all his mules, Sally was the most agreeable. Nothing seemed to bother her. The mule was slower than his other mules, but she bore his weight without complaint. Saddling up his mule, Bear was reminded of a story an old trapper told him: "I know this sounds outlandish, but I swear it's true. One day, I encountered a man who had sunk up to his neck in quicksand. I asked the man if he needed any help. He just smiled and said, 'No, thank you, I'm riding a damn good mule.' And sure enough, as I watched, his head began to move. Soon, I could see his shoulder, then his upper body, and finally, his mule appeared. That animal emerged from the quicksand and heehawed. The old timer just smiled and rode off."

"Well, girl, let's try and stay out of the quicksand."

Lightning streaked across the sky as Bear and Sally headed toward Eric's ranch. Reaching Eric's and Sara's house, Bear was shocked to see the flood waters swirling around the barn. The barn's double doors had been torn off by the storm. Bear urged his mule forward and led Sally into the barn. Inside was chaos as the chicken, pigs, their milk cows, and two mules were in full panic. The river's water now covered the barn's floor by several inches. Bear realized he couldn't carry all the animals to the safety of his barn. So he shooed the pigs and chickens out into the storm.

"Don't know if the chickens and pigs can swim. So, whether they can survive this flood is anybody's guess."

Bear looped ropes over the mules and cow, "Okay, easy, does it." said Bear as he mounted Sally and led the animals from the barn. They had only gone twenty feet when a lightning bolt struck a large oak tree near Eric's house.

The mules and cow panicked as the lightning, followed by a loud clap of thunder, split the tree in two, sending the tree crashing to the ground. The ropes burned Bear's hands as he struggled to hold the rope. Sally instinctively dug her hooves into the muddy ground and pulled. Unfortunately, the effect of Sally's strength and the mules and cow pulling in the opposite direction yanked Bear out of his saddle. Sally lunged up the hill free of her burden, leaving Bear sitting in the mud and Eric's animals running for their lives.

"Damn!" cussed Bear as the animals disappeared into the fog and rain. Slipping and sliding, Bear finally made it back up the hill, where Sally waited for him. The mule looked at Bear with her big brown eyes as if to say, "I told you that was a bad idea."

"Alright, gal. Now that we made a mess of rescuing Eric's livestock, let's see if we can find my son."

Bear figured the horses that broke out of the corral would have headed for higher ground. So Bear climbed back into the saddle and rode toward the foothills. The storm continued to pelt Bear and Sally with rain that was sometimes driven sideways by the relentless wind. Worse, as the temperature dropped, the rain turned to sleet and hail.

"I believe this is what the old timers called a hurricane."

Ever since moving to Texas, Bear had heard horror stories about hurricanes. These monster storms would gather moisture from the Gulf of Mexico and roar into Texas, destroying everything in its path.

"I hope Eric is smart enough to find shelter and wait out the storm."

Bear thought he knew the land around his ranch like the back of his hand, but now, he wasn't so sure. After another hour, Bear decided that his son was either holed up in one of the many caves that dotted the foothills or had returned to the ranch. "Let's go home, girl," said Bear as he turned the mule back down the hillside.

Suddenly, Bear saw Eric's horse emerge from the storm. He kicked Sally into a fast trot and quickly caught up with the Chesnut mare. The horse had a wild look of fear in her eyes. For a moment, Bear thought the mare would bolt and disappear back into the storm. But fortunately, the horse was too worn out. It just stood shaking with its legs spread apart. Bear slid from his saddle and, speaking softly, approached the mare.

"Easy now, girl. It looks like you've had quite a fright."

Bear ran his hand over the horse. The poor animal was covered in scratches. Her right front leg had an ugly cut that ran from the horse's shoulder to halfway down its leg.

"Where's Eric, huh? Is he alright? Damn, I sure wish you could talk."

The thought of his son lying injured in this storm chilled the big man to his bones. Bear had faced many dangers as a mountain man in Wyoming and now in Texas. But the prospect of his son hurt and battling this storm alone was almost more than Bear could handle. He stood next to Eric's horse, debating what to do next as the sleet and wind lashed out at him. Finally, his mind made up; Bear grabbed the mare's reins and mounted his mule.

"Eric will never forgive me if I leave his horse out here to die in the storm."

The ride downhill to the ranch was a constant battle with the elements. The driving sleet had changed back to rain, but the wind continued to howl. The rain had turned the trail into a slippery slide, and it was all Bear could do to keep his mule and Eric's horse from tumbling down the slope. Once again, the mules' surefootedness saved the day, and they reached the valley floor without incident.

The fog had finally lifted, and Bear was shocked to see that his cabin and Eric's were separated by raging water. *"Eric's cabin looks like an island in the middle of a river,"* he thought as he approached his house.

Bear rode straight to his barn. Dismounting, he opened the barn door and led the animals inside.

"There now, you're safe. Let's get you dried off and look

at that cut." Bear wanted nothing more than to turn right around and search for Eric. However, he also knew that the animals came first. Plus, he needed a change of clothes and supplies.

"I trust Eric's ability to take care of himself. Besides, it would do me no good to go back out in the storm without proper provisions."

Since his son was old enough to walk, Bear had taught him how to survive in the wilds with nothing but his wits. By the time Eric was twelve years old, Bear decided he was ready for his test. Giving his son an old skinning knife, Bear blindfolded him, and then they rode far up into the mountains. Once there, Bear took off his son's blindfold and said, "Before a Shoshone boy can join the men on a hunt, he must first pass this test. Using only this rusty knife, you must build a shelter, make fire, and kill a deer. I will come back in ten days. Remember what I told you about keeping calm and trusting what you've learned."

Bear hugged his son and, without another word, rode off. Ten days later, he returned to find Eric scrapping a deer hide by his leanto. Strips of venison were drying near a fire while a hunk of meat was roasting on a spit. His son, bare to the chest, tanned and lean, smiled broadly. Ten days ago, Bear had said goodbye to a boy, and now he welcomed a young man into the brotherhood of mountain men. Bear held that image in his mind as he rubbed down his mule.

Once he had taken care of Sally and Eric's horse, Bear returned to the cabin.

"Goodness, did you have to roll in the mud? You stay right there and strip. I'll not have you mucky up my clean floor!" ordered Waity.

Sara giggled, "Come along, children, I'll read you a story."

Waity waited until the children and Sara were out of earshot, "It's bad out there, isn't it?"

"Yep, and it'll get worse. Farther up the mountains, it's snowing. Down here in the valley, we're surrounded by flood water, and it's still raining."

"Did you find Eric?'

"Not yet. I did get the animals out of Eric's barn. I was leading the mules and their milk cow back here when a lightning bolt struck that old oak tree and spooked the animals. I hope they had the good sense to seek higher ground."

"And Eric?" asked Waity.

"I couldn't find him, but I did find his horse. The mare had a cut on its right leg, so I brought her back to our barn."

"But no, Eric?"

"I'm afraid not. By the time I reached the ranch, I was soaked and cold. I figure I get a change of clothes, have something hot to drink, and head back out."

Waity sadly nodded her head. "What are you going to tell Sara?"

"The truth. Eric is a skilled frontiersman who knows

how to survive in any situation. He's probably holed up in some nice, dry cave, waiting for the rain to stop."

"I sure hope you're right," replied Waity.

"Me too, Luv, Me too."

Chet appeared at the door as Bear was pulling on his buckskin shirt. For a moment, Chet stared at the big man's upper body. Bear's chest and back were covered with scars from knife fights, bullets, and the occasional teeth marks of a human or animal. Chet cleared his throat.

"Did you find your son?"

"Not yet, but I will. I was just telling my wife he's camped out in some cave, taking a nap."

Chet laughed, "I'm sure that's the case. What about Brett Simon?"

"Didn't see a trace of him either," replied Bear.

"I sure wish I could go with you."

"No worries," said Bear. "With me gone, I feel better having you here."

"What's that supposed to mean?" huffed Waity. "Are you saying Sara and I can't take care of ourselves? You forget that Sara is a crack shot, and I'm pretty good with a gun myself."

"Remember how I picked off those pirates?" said Sara, entering the room.

"Of course," replied Bear, "It's just, that Brett Simon swore he get me and my family because I killed his boy."

"But," said Chet, "I heard that was a fair fight."

"It was. Simon's gang bushwacked me. I fired back and hit his son. Truth be told, it was a lucky shot."

"Don't take offense, Chet," said Sara, "With Bear and my husband always away, Waity and I are used to looking out for ourselves."

Bear shook his head, "As you can see, Chet, marrying strong-willed women is not all it's cracked up to be." Everyone laughed at Bear's comment.

"Now, I see why Bear and his family are so respected," Chet thought.

Waity handed Bear some deer jerky, pemmican, a hunk of salt pork, coffee, and a jug of whiskey. "Time's a wasting, Luv. When you get back, we can all celebrate. But now you have work to do, finding my son and Sara's husband!" Waity gave Bear a peck on his bearded cheek and shooed him out the door.

Bear's two Irish Wolfhounds were waiting for him on the porch. "Thor, come! Odin, stay! Guard Waity."

Thor wagged his tail and looked up at Bear. Odin, looking rejected, sat on his haunches until Bear said, "Stay,"

The Irish Wolfhound took one last longing look at Bear, then turned and stood next to Waity. "That's a good boy," soothed Waity as she scratched Odin's head. "Stay here where it's nice and dry."

3

BACK INTO THE STORM

Bear hated to saddle up Sally. But of all his mules, Sally was the most tireless, dependable, and sure-footed. The mule seemed to relish the challenge of rough terrain. Bear laid the saddle blanket on Sally's back. "Sorry, gal, but we have to go back out into the storm."

The mule seemed to understand as she turned her head and looked at Bear. "I know it's nasty out there, but we must find Eric."

Next, Bear saddled another mule and strapped down the canvas cover they used on the wagon. "Might come in handy."

Bear led Sally and the other mule outside and shut the barn doors. He pulled this felt hat lower on his head and, with one last wave to Waity, ducked his head behind Sally's neck. "Alright, let's go find Eric."

The wind and rain lashed Bear like a bullwhip, and soon, the mountain man, his hound, and mules were soaked. "Seen worse, haven't we, Sally?"

His mule answered the question with a shake of her head, "No, you're right. This is the worst storm we've ever seen. Those blizzards up north could last for days, but at least you didn't get soaked to the skin."

In Bear's mind, there was only one direction his son would go in, *"If'n I was Eric, I head for higher ground. That's probably where the horses skedaddled to."*

Bear retraced his trail until he reached the foothills. Then, he rode slowly to the right. Bear planned to sweep the area, hoping to find any signs of Eric and the horses.

"The rain has nearly washed out the trail, but hopefully, thirty horses will still leave something behind."

After hours of slipping and sliding, Bear feared the rain had washed away any tracks the horses left. But then he saw several piles of horse dung.

"Well, looky here. I knew that many horses had to leave a sign or two. It looks like they rested here for a while before moving on. Now, I have to figure out which direction they went. I recall a small meadow with the sweetest green grass and red clover. Eric and I would bring the ponies to the field every summer."

Finally, the rain let up a bit, and the wind died down, making it easier for Bear to locate the small meadow.

"Well, there you are? But where is Eric?"

The horses had gathered together under a small stand of trees in the middle of the field. A few brave ponies had ventured away from the herd and were contently eating the grass and clover. Bear scanned the area, looking for Eric. Not seeing him, and with darkness descending, Bear was forced to stop and find shelter.

"This looks as good a spot as any." Bear led Sally into a grove of spruce trees. Then, using the canvas tarp, he made himself a shelter.

"Let's see if I can get a fire going."

Every mountain man knew that after knowing how to tie a tourniquet or mend a broken bone, fire starting was an essential skill. Without fire, a man couldn't stay warm, keep wolves away, and cook a meal.

A mountain man needed to know how to start a fire in any condition. Because of this, Bear always carried a fire-starting kit rolled up in his bedroll. So, after erecting his shelter, Bear unrolled the oilskin cloth that kept his blanket, extra set of clothes, and fire-making kit dry. The oilskin also served as a ground cloth where Bear would lay his blanket.

Next, Bear broke off the dead branches from the spruce trees. The branches sheltered from the rain by the spruce trees were, for the most part, dry. After gathering the wood, Bear took out his kit.

Bear's fire-starting kit consisted of flint, a small tin containing charred pieces of cloth, and tinder. Carefully, Bear placed a bundle of tinder on the oilskin. Then he tucked a piece of charred cloth into the tinder. Finally, he pulled his knife and, bending low to block the wind, struck the flint with the back of the blade. It took several attempts before a spark landed on the cloth and began to burn. Quickly, Bear scooped the tinder and gently blew.

"Come on now, burn!"

Bear blew again, and a whisp of smoke curled up from the tinder ball. One more puff and the tinder burst into flames. Bear placed the burning bundle on the ground and laid some dry pine on top. Once the pine was burning, he laid more and bigger sticks on the fire until it burned brightly.

"Now to boil me some coffee."

Bear sipped the hot coffee he had laced with the whiskey as he fried the salt pork. Bear shared his supper with Thor. After eating, he let the fire burn down, rolled up in his blanket, and slept with Thor tucked beside him.

Morning dawned, and with it, more rain. Bear packed his gear and, saddling Sally, headed further into the foothills. By noon, he had made his way deep into the small hills and ravines that ringed the Franklin Mountains.

"I know you're here somewhere, son."

Bear pulled his pistol, fired a shot, and held his breath as he listened. He didn't have to wait long as his shot was answered by the boom of Eric's rifle.

"Alleluia, that's my boy!"

Thor barked, and Bear pulled sharply at Sally's reins, "Come girl, you can rest as soon as we find Eric."

Bear rode in the direction of the rifle shot. As he got closer, he yelled, "Eric!"

His shout was immediately answered, "Pa, I'm over here under the rock ledge!"

Hearing Eric's voice, Thor ran ahead of Bear.

Bear headed in the direction of the outcropping. As he did, Bear remembered the first time he and Eric discovered this meadow and the ledge.

"Pa, that ledge looks like a good place to camp."

"Yep, especially if those dark clouds bless us with rain."

Eric was the first to reach the rock shelter. Bear was removing their gear when his son shouted excitedly, "Pa, you got to see this place!"

Ducking under the ledge, Bear looked where Eric was pointing. The ledge opened to a shallow cave. On the walls were figures of hunters stalking buffalo.

"Well, ain't that something," said Bear. "I've heard of these drawings, but this is my first time seeing them."

"How old do you figure the drawings are?"

"Hard to tell, son. The Yaquis called these people Anasaz or ancient ones."

"I wonder what happened to them."

"Probably what happens to all of us sooner or later. We die out or are conquered by a stronger tribe."

Bear could smell woodsmoke as he got closer and

smiled, *"That's my boy. Even in a flood, he manages to build a fire."*

Reaching the ledge, Bear peered in. His son was leaning against the cave wall, wearing a big smile, as he patted Thor's head.

"Ain't you suppose to be herding up the horses?"

"I was, but then my horse slipped and broke my leg."

That's when Bear noticed Eric was wearing a splint on his right leg. "Sara's been worried sick about you."

"Yeah, I bet. So how's my farm? When I left, the river had overflowed its banks."

"I hate to tell you this. But, the flood had already reached the barn. I shooed out the pigs and chickens. I tried to lead your milk cow and mules to my barn when a lightning bolt hit a nearby tree, and the animals scattered."

"Well, hopefully, they survived. Hey, you didn't happen to bring any food? I'm starved."

"Sure, I got some jerky, pemmican, salt pork, coffee, and whiskey."

"I'd like the whiskey first. This leg is barking at me."

Bear handed his son the whiskey jug, then examined the leg. "Well, you did a fine job of setting the bone. Now, it's just a matter of letting the bone heal."

"Yep, but first, we must figure out how I will get back home."

"If it keeps raining, maybe we can build a raft and float home." Joked Bear.

"Ha, we might just do that. How's the horses?"

"Near as I could tell, they're all there."

"And my mare? I remembered the cave and thought I'd climb in to get dry, but the mare slipped on the loose rock and fell. I tumbled from the saddle and broke my leg. It took a while, had to stop because of the pain, but finally, I made it to the cave. I think someone else uses the cave because I found a supply of firewood and built the fire."

"I see you've been busy drawing on the walls."

"It took my mind off the leg. I figured I'd add my story to the other drawings, and who knows, a thousand years from now, someone will look at the pictures and wonder who drew them."

"Hmm, I'll rustle up some grub, then we have to figure out how to get you home."

As Bear prepared their meal, he told Eric about the Texas Ranger and his run-in with Brett Simons.

"I recall Chet, a young, rangy fellow with a big nose and hands."

"Yep, that's *Henderson. He won't win no beauty contest, But he's honest as the day is long."

"So, Pa, you figure Brett's come gunning for you?"

"Yep, I do. I didn't want to worry about your Ma or Sara, but the only reason he's in the area is to kill me. Stealing those cattle from Gordon Fisher was just a happy accident."

"Then we better get home quick!"

"Nobody's moving around in this storm, Eric. Come morning, we'll head out, but for now, eat and sleep are what the doctor ordered."

"And whiskey?"

"Aye, and whiskey,"

4

BRETT SIMON

B rett Simon swore and tossed the cards on the barn floor.

"Another losing hand?"

"Shut up, Jake! Deal me in while I take a leak. This time, give me some cards I can work with."

Brett stood at the open barn door and relieved himself. He buttoned up and turned back to the three men. "Hey, Brett, did you hear what the old timer said when a man asked him if it would ever stop raining?"

Brett stared at his younger brother. "You half-wit. I'm sick and tired of your dumb jokes!"

"I don't mean no harm. I'm just trying to lighten things up."

"Go ahead," smiled Ray Denton, "I'd like to hear the answer. What did the old timer say?"

"It always has!" laughed Jake,

"Get it? The old timer said...,"

"Just shut your yap and deal!" growled Clayton Brown, the third member of Brett's gang.

"Clayton's right! Deal or drop out of the game!" snarled Brett.

"Drop out of the game? But I'm winning!" whined Jake.

"For the love of Mike, deal!" yelled Brett.

"Alright, Jeeze!"

Jake dealt each man five cards. Brett picked up his cards, *"Five cards and not a face card or pair."* Disgusted, Brett waited for the other men to make their move.

"I'll open for two," said Clayton as he slid two silver dollars to the center.

Everyone placed their bets, but when it was Brett's turn, he slapped down his cards.

"That's it, I'm out."

Pulling a plug of tobacco from his pocket, he cut off a piece and stuck it in his mouth. Two hours ago, the gang had taken shelter in the tumbled-down barn. Half the roof had caved in, and there were gaps in the walls where boards had been torn off. Still, it was better than nothing. They had even found an old cast iron stove. It didn't heat up the drafty barn, but after rigging a clothesline above the stove, it was hot enough to dry their wet clothes.

Brett stood at the open door and stared out into the storm. Behind him, Clayton started arguing with Jake. "I know you're dealing from the bottom of the deck!"

"No, I ain't," protested Jake. "You're just mad because you're losing."

"I'm losing because you're cheating!" shouted Clayton, "And you know what happens to a man who cheats, don't you?"

Brett whirled around, pistol in hand, and fired the bullet, hitting Clayton squarely in the chest and tossing his body backward. Jake and Ray sat dumbfounded. Brett stomped over to Jake and ripped the deck from his hands. He turned the deck over and peeled two Aces from the bottom of the deck. Brett slapped the Aces on the floor.

"Clayton was right. You were cheating."

"Well, maybe a little," admitted Jake.

"There's no little, you idiot! If you weren't my brother, it would be you lying on the floor, not Clayton! Now, hand me those cards!"

Denton and Jake gave Brett their cards. Brett walked over to the rusty potbelly stove, opened the door, and tossed the cards into the flames."

"Now get some sleep! As soon as the rain lets up, we're out of here."

Brett returned to the door, "I'm coming for you, Willis!" he hissed.

It was still raining the next day, but Brett decided to leave the barn's shelter. His brother, Jake, seemed to have forgotten what happened last night.

"Do you know where Bear Willis ranch is located?" asked Denton.

"Not exactly, only that it's in a long, narrow valley, bordered by a small river on one side and the Franklin mountains on the other."

"So, if you don't know where Willis lives, how will you find him?" asked Jake.

"Because dummy, a man with Willis's reputation has got to be well known. We'll ask at the next farmhouse."

Riding alongside the brothers, Ray Denton was beginning to think he made a big mistake. Denton was still dealing with Brett's killing of Clayton Brown. *Brett's desire for revenge is going to get us all killed. I agreed to go with Brett because he promised we would get rich, rustling cattle. But all he cares about is killing Bear Willis.*

An hour later, the three outlaws came upon a small log cabin. Smoke curling out of the chimney meant that someone was inside.

Brett halted under a large tree. "See that cabin? The people inside don't know it, but they will help us trap Bear Willis."

Jake was going to ask a question, but Brett silenced him with one look. "We should be able to sneak up on the cabin without being seen. Denton, go around back and make sure no one escapes. Jake and I will bust in the front door."

Ray Denton did as he was told. Reaching the rear door of the cabin, he drew his gun and waited. Seconds later, he heard a woman scream, followed by gunfire. The outlaw climbed down and entered the cabin. A young woman sat on the floor, cradling her husband. The bullet hole in the middle of the man's head left no doubt that he was dead.

Nearby, a baby cried. The child lay on a blanket near the fire. Tears flowed from the young wife's eyes as she looked at the outlaws, "Why? What did my husband do to deserve this?"

"He made the mistake of going for his rifle," scoffed Brett.

"The gun isn't even loaded," yelled the woman. "I won't allow loaded guns in my house!"

"That so," said Brett, "Then he deserved to be shot for being stupid."

The woman began to wail. Brett reached down and yanked her up by her long brown hair. "You do know Bear Willis, don't you?"

"Everyone knows Mr. Willis," sobbed the woman.

"Then you know where he lives?"

The woman sniffed, "He and his son have a ranch about twenty miles to the north."

"Good, here's a five-dollar gold piece for your troubles."

Brett slapped the coin on the kitchen table, "Pretty gal like you should have no problem finding another man. Of course, you can come with us. My brother is looking for a woman, ain't ya, Jake?"

"I sure am," stuttered Jake, "After we kill Bear Willis, we'll rob a few banks and then retire to Mexico."

"You're all fools!" Screamed the woman. "I hope Bear Willis carves out your heart while it's still beating."

"Bloodthirsty little tart, ain't she?" laughed Brett.

They walked out of the small house and back into the rain. Suddenly, Denton stopped and shouted, "I didn't sign up for this! You told me we would get rich rustling cattle. You didn't say anything about killing innocent folks!"

"You're right, I didn't," admitted Brett, "So feel free to leave, and no hard feelings."

The outlaw spat on the ground, "That's just what I'm going to do."

Ray Denton turned his back and started walking back to his horse. He only got halfway when Brett fired, hitting Ray between the shoulders and killing him instantly.

"Take his guns and horse," ordered Brett.

Jake did as he was told. Then, the two brothers mounted their horses and rode in the direction of Bear Willis's ranch.

5

LONG RIDE HOME

Bear woke to the sound of rain, *"Still raining, but not as hard as yesterday."*

Bear stood and stretched the kinks out of his back. "

Must be tough, getting old," joked Eric.

"I see you're feeling better," said Bear.

"Not really. The leg hurts like heck, and I didn't get much sleep. You slept right through a violent storm. The wind howled like the devil himself was rising out of hell."

"Well, the storm has let up. So I boil some coffee, and we'll eat a cold breakfast. Then, I make the travois, and we'll take you home to Sara and the kids."

"I imagine Sara and Mom are worried sick."

"Women are born to worry. It's their nature. But Sara

and Ma know we'll be alright. After all, it's just a little rain shower."

"Little rain shower? I'll be lucky if it hasn't washed away my farm."

"We can always rebuild, son. Just as long as the women and children are safe. That's all that really matters."

After coffee and some venison jerky, Bear began fashioning a travois from the canvas tarp. First, Bear cut six saplings. The two longest poles would serve as the frame to which the smaller poles would be lashed. When done, the travois resembled a long triangle, sturdy enough to support Eric but light enough for the mule to haul. Then Bear tied the canvas to the frame and attached the travois to the mule.

"Ready to give it a try, son?"

"Yeah, let's go."

Bear put his arm around Eric's waist and helped him limp out of the cave. The travois bent under Eric's weight, but it held. "Ready, son?"

"Yep,"

"I'll take it slow, but it'll still be rough. Yell out if you need to rest."

"I will, Pa."

"Okay, then, here we go."

Bear nudged Sally forward. He had tied a loop around the other mule and attached the other end of the rope to his saddle horn. As the two mules moved down the trail, Bear turned to watch. The mule hid most of the Eric and the travois, but Bear could see the end of the wooden poles as they dragged along the ground.

"So far, so good," Bear thought, *"It'll be a slow trip, but at least the rain stopped."*

After a few miles, Bear halted and returned to check on Eric.

"How's the ride?"

"I think I've jarred loose half of my teeth," grinned his son, "and I think some of the lashings need tightening."

Bear checked all the bindings and tightened the loose ones. "That should hold for a few more miles. Now that we are off the side of the mountain, the going will be easier."

Bear climbed back in the saddle, *"At this rate, it'll take us at least two days to get home."*

Bear and Eric continued up the trail, stopping to rest the mules every few miles and tighten the lashings. By midday, they had traveled only ten miles. As they rode, Eric and Bear were amazed at the damage left by the storm. Old trees had been uprooted and tossed about like matchsticks. Other trees had been reduced to kindling by a lightning bolt. But the worst destruction was from the flooding. More than once, they had to detour around a lake formed when a small stream flooded its banks.

When they finally stopped for the night, both men and animals were exhausted. The constant jerking of the travois had caused Eric's broken leg to start throbbing. This and being strapped to the travois taxed even Eric's youthful energy. Eric tried to lift himself up but collapsed on the wooden frame travois.

"Take it easy, son. Let me lift you out." Bear put one arm under Eric's shoulders and the other under his son's knees and lifted Eric like he was some ragdoll. Bear carried Eric over to his bedroll and laid him down.

"After supper, I make you a crutch so you can get about without me carrying you."

"How much further?" asked Eric.

"I figure another day, barring any detours." Replied Bear.

"I sure wish there was some way of letting Sara and Mom know we're okay."

"Yep, that would be nice. I remember my first wife, Little Sparrow, telling me that when I'm away from her, I should look at the North Star and know she was staring at the same star. Somehow, that made the times apart a little more bearable. It's something your mom and I still do."

"That's a nice thought," commented Eric as he gazed at the North Star.

6

WOLF HUNT

Well, the children are finally asleep," said Waity, sitting heavily in the rocking chair. She had joined Sara and Odin out on the front porch. It was the first time they could go outside without getting soaked in several days.

"I'm worried about Eric and Dad," sighed Sara.

"Me too," admitted Waity, "I keep reminding myself that Bear and Eric are experienced mountain men. Except for the storm, there should be nothing to cause them any harm."

"I sure hope you're right," replied Sara.

"I never told you this. But you remember us talking about Little Sparrow?"

"Yes, Bear's first wife, the Shoshone."

"Yes, sadly, I never met Little Sparrow, but from everything Bear told me, she was quite a woman. Anyway, Little Sparrow claimed that Bear was protected by his spirit guide, a great grizzly bear, and because of this, Bear could not die."

"Does this grizzly protect Bear's son?"

"I'm sure it does. One of the things Bear and I do when we're apart is to gaze up at the North Star at night. It comforts me that no matter how far away we are, we're both looking at the same star."

"Thanks, Waity, I'll try that."

Both women were deep in their thoughts when Chet Henderson limped out the door. "I hope I ain't disturbing you ladies, but after being cooped up in the house for days, it sure is nice to be outside in the fresh air."

"Yes, it is," replied Waity, "I love how fresh the air smells after a rain."

Chet grimaced as he eased himself down on a bench.

"That leg bothering you tonight?" asked Sara.

"Yes, ma'am, it is, and the wound is still leaky blood."

"It's no wonder," said Waity, "You need to rest, not be playing tag with the young'uns."

"Yes, I suppose you're right. But I get tired of just lying in that bed."

"Tomorrow, I'll look at your leg and change the dressing."

"Thank you, Waity, and you too, Sara. You've both been very kind."

"We're just glad you found us. As bad as the storm was, you could have ridden right by the ranch."

"Yes, I was lucky," replied Chet, "I guess someone upstairs was watching over me."

"Someone or something," smiled Sara.

"What do you mean?" asked Chet.

"Maybe Pa's spirit guide showed you the way."

"Maybe it did," agreed Chet. "By the way, shouldn't we hear from Bear soon?"

"We should," agreed Waity, "But knowing Bear, he and Eric probably decided to do a little hunting while they're out."

"Since I joined the Rangers, I've heard one story after another about your husband," said Chet. "If even half the tales are true, you're husband is an amazing man."

"Ha," laughed Waity, "My husband always seems to find trouble, or trouble finds him. So, whatever tall tales you've heard are probably true."

Chet yawned, "Excuse me, ladies, I best get some rest. I want to leave soon before Captain Wallace charges me with desertion."

Chet returned to the house, "Mr. Henderson is a fine young man," commented Sara.

"Yes, he is," replied Waity. "If he lives long enough, he may even find a good girl to marry him."

"What do you mean, live long enough?"

"Rangering is a dangerous occupation. Between renegade

Indians, Mexican banditos crossing the border, and outlaws, a Texas Rangedr's chances of living past thirty are slim. Just look at what happened to Chet. He was ambushed, and although he escaped, Chet was wounded. If he hadn't found our cabin, young Mr. Henderson would have bled to death."

"We live in violent times, Sara. Life on the frontier isn't for the faint-hearted. Bear and I could have decided to live in a city. But we would have been miserable. Can you picture Bear Willis working as a clerk behind a desk?"

Sara laughed, "Goodness no,"

"Neither could I. Freedom is a heavy load. It comes at great cost and sacrifice. However, for Bear and myself, there is no better life."

"Eric and I feel the same way, " replied Sara, "Hopefully, the sacrifices we make today will ensure our children a better life."

"Let's hope so." Waity took one last look at the North Star and whispered, "Stay safe, Luv, and come home to me."

The next morning, despite Waity's advice that he rest. Chet was up early and in the barn brushing down his horse. "You ain't planning on leaving, are you?"

Chet looked up at Sara as she entered the barn. "My horse needs some exercise."

"I'm sure it does, and I'd be happy to ride her down the trail a bit."

"Thanks, Sara, but I'd rather do it myself. Waity changed the bandages today and said I was a fast healer. So I don't think a little sauntered would hurt me."

"Alright, just don't overdo it, and take Odin with you. He's getting fat and lazy hanging around the cabin."

"Alright, just as long as Odin won't eat me."

Sara laughed at Chet's joke. She was beginning to like the big, homely Texas Ranger. Of course, her only love was Eric. But Chet Henderson had a certain boyish charm that made a woman want to mother him.

Chet rode slowly, nursing his wounded leg. *"I'll ride along the river and see what damages the storm caused."*

As he rode, Chet thought of his childhood and how different it was from the Willis children.

"Those younguns don't know how lucky they are, having a mother and father who love them."

It wasn't that his mother and father hadn't loved him. His father died in a coal mining accident when Chet was twelve, and two years later, Chet's mom died of TB. When asked about his childhood, Chet would shrug his shoulders and say, "It was a hardscrabble life."

"Rangering is my life now," he thought, *"It ain't never had real friends till I joined the Rangers. Hopefully, I can also count Bear and his family as friends."*

Thinking about his life, Chet rode on, and the miles slipped away. It wasn't until he heard the Irish Wolfhound growl that he focused on the present. Chet looked at Odin, shocked at the big hound's appearance change. For most of the ride, Odin, free from the confines of the cabin, would run back and forth, sniffing at every down tree and watering a bush to leave his mark. But now, the hound had transformed into a savage hunter. His hair stood straight up on his back. Odin's large mouth was drawn back, revealing his fangs and a deep guttural growl rumbled up from his gut.

The hound's body was like a wound spring, and his eyes were focused on something in the distance. Chet squinted, "Wolves!" Ahead were two wolves feating on the carcass of a dead cow. Chet remembered what Bear had told him about the Irish Wolfhounds.

"They were bred to run down and kill wolves, and that's why no wolves are left in Ireland."

At the time, Chet thought Bear was pulling his leg. But now, looking at the beast beside him, Chet realized that the mountain man was telling him the truth. Suddenly, Odin launched himself in the direction of the wolves. Realizing he was helpless to stop Odin, Chet pulled his rifle from its leather sheath and kicked his horse into a gallop.

The wolves looked up as the huge hound bore down on them. The wolves had never seen a hound this big or this fierce. This was their territory, and except for the occasional bear, the wolves had no enemies but man. Seeing a massive Irish Wolfhound rushing toward them was a new experience. But another predator, no matter how big, challenging them for the dead cow would be in for the fight of its life.

Chet raised his rifle, planning to shoot the wolves. But

he needn't have bothered as Odin, without breaking stride, slammed into the first wolf. Both animals went down in a tumble of teeth and claws.

"He's a goner for sure," thought Chet. But then, to his amazement, Odin stood! He had the wolf's throat in his massive jaws. The Irish Wolfhound shook the wolf like one would shake a ragdoll. When Odin finally released the wolf, it was dead. Seeing what happened to his companion, the second wolf turned tail and ran. The last Chet saw of Odin and the wolf, they disappeared over a rise in the trail.

"If I hadn't seen it with my own eyes, I wouldn't have believed it."

Urging his horse forward, Chet rode after the hound. Finally, a mile down the trail, he saw Odin looping toward him. The hound's face and chest were splattered with blood. At first, Chet thought the blood was Odin's. But as the hound got closer, he realized that Odin was unharmed. Odin ran over to Chet and sat on its haunches. If not for the blood, you would think the hound had just returned from a run.

"Damn, Odin, you're really something. But now we best be getting back to the ranch."

7

A SON FOR A SON

Hold up, Jake. Is that smoke I smell?"

"Yeah, it smells like someone's cooking supper. Maybe it's Bear Willis's place. Do you think he'll invite us in for dinner?"

"If it is Willis' farm, I don't think so, but then he won't have a choice."

They rode through a grove of trees. In the distance was a well-built log cabin. Next to the house was a barn and several outbuildings.

"Looks like the mountain man has done alright for himself," said Brett.

"Shame. It's all going to come crashing down," laughed Jake.

"Listen, you fool, don't do anything stupid. Willis is a

dangerous man. Just follow my lead and obey my orders, and we'll be okay."

"Why not wait and bushwack him when he goes to the outhouse?"

"Because I want to look into his eyes as he dies and spit on his grave."

Jake laughed, "I can't wait to see that."

"Just shut up. We're almost there. Tie up the horses to that tree and follow me."

The two brothers crept closer to the cabin. "They must be eating," whispered Brett. "Go around to the back door, and when I kick in the front. I want you to enter from the back."

"I hear Willis has a pretty wife, maybe..,"

"Just do what you're told, and keep it in your pants!"

Brett watched his brother walk around to the back of the log cabin. "The idiot, if he messes up, I'll skin him alive."

Brett counted to thirty. Then he grabbed the door latch and, using his shoulder, shoved open the door. Sara and Waity never had a chance to defend themselves. Waity and Sara sat around the kitchen table with their children. Little Rose screamed at the sight of the black-bearded man holding a rifle in the doorway.

"Nobody moves, and you won't get hurt!" shouted Brett as his brother entered the room. Brett looked around, "Where's Bear Willis?"

"Wouldn't you like to know," scoffed Waity. "I wouldn't want to be you when he gets back."

It angered Brett that neither Waity nor Sara showed any fear. If anything, they showed contempt for the intruders.

"So, Bear ain't home, huh?" said Jake, licking his lips.

"Shut up, brother," ordered Brett.

Waity's eyes narrowed, "You're the Simon brothers?"

"That's right, sweetie. Your husband kilt my son, and now we're here to take one of yours."

"Over my dead body," screamed Waity. As she moved closer to Charles.

"I'll make it easy for you. If you don't give us your son. I'll start shooting the other children until you change your mind."

"It's alright, Mama. I ain't afraid, I'll go with them."

Waity, seeing that she had no choice, took off her old, red shawl. Then she bet down and wrapped it around Charles. "Do you remember the story about Hansel and Gretel?"

"Yes, Mama,"

"And remember how they used bread crumbs to find their way home?"

"Yes,"

"Pretend this shawl is a loaf of bread and the yarn is the crumbs. Do you understand?'

Waity looked into her son's eyes. At first, Charles looked confused, then smiled, "Bread crumbs, yes, Mama, I understand."

"Good boy, I love you. Be brave, Charles. Your father will come for you."

"I know, Mama."

"Come on, enough of the tears. Let's go, boy!"

"My name is Charles, not boy!"

"Well, Mr. Charles, ain't you the smart one."

Brett grabbed Charles by the scuff of his neck and led him out the door. He reached the horses and turned to see where Jake was.

"Jake! Get out here!"

Jake exited the cabin with a big slice of apple pie in his dirty hands. The syrup dripped between his fingers as he shoved the pie into his mouth.

"That was damn good pie," said Jake, licking the sweet syrup from his fingers.

"How can someone so stupid be my brother? Get your butt into the saddle. Before Willis shows up!"

"Are we going to Californy now?" asked Jake.

"Yes, we are going to California." Said Brett as he lifted Charles onto his horse."

"Hey, California, here we come."

"Shut up!" scolded Brett.

As Chet returned to the ranch, he knew he was in for a scolding from Waity. The horse ride had reopened his wound. Blood soaked the bandages and his pant leg.

"I should have taken it slower and not raced off after Odin."

Chet was still in awe of the Irish Wolfhound's speed and strength in killing the wolves. *"Someday, I'd like to get me one of these hounds."*

As Chet rode closer to Bear's ranch house, he could see something was wrong. Waity and Sara stood on the porch, yelling at each other while the children sat at their mothers' feet, crying.

"What the devil is going on!"

Ignoring the ache in his leg, he spurred his horse into a gallop. Reaching the house, Chet jerked his horse to a stop and limped to the women.

"What's the matter?" asked Chet.

"Brett and Jake Simon have taken Charles!" cried Waity.

"The Simons were here?"

"Yes, and they kidnapped my boy."

"But why?" asked Chet

"Brett Simon said it was because Bear shot and killed his son. He plans to raise the boy as his own."

"That's terrible," exclaimed Chet. "I'll go after them!"

Chet turned and, putting his weight on his injured leg, nearly fell down.

"You ain't going anywhere," said Waity.

"Waity's determined to ride after Charles," said Sara, "I've tried to stop her, but Waity's mind is made up."

"Waity, this is crazy," said Chet. "One woman against two hardened killers? You wouldn't stand a chance. You stay here with your family, and I'll go."

"You ain't going anywhere," ordered Waity. "Just look at

your leg. That wound has opened up. If you go off after Brett and his brother, you could lose your leg and maybe even your life."

"Waity, I'm sure Bear and Eric will be here soon. It would be best if you stayed here." Pleaded Sara.

"Sara's right," commented Chet, "Wait for your husband."

"What, and miss a chance of catching up with them and freeing my son? You heard them, Sara. Brett said they were going to California. Once the brothers get into the mountains, we'll never find them."

"Exactly, why you should wait for Bear."

"Listen, you two, I know you mean well, but my mind is made up. I may not be as good a tracker as my husband, but I'm better than most men. Sara, you know I can ride and shoot. Together, side by side, Bear and I have fought Indians, pirates, and outlaws. There's only two Simons, and one of them is a half-wit."

Chet looked at Sara, who sadly shook her head. "Fine, Waity, go, but please be careful and promise that you won't make a move on the brothers until Bear and Eric show up."

"I can't make that promise, Sara. If the situation presents itself, I'll do what I must to save Charles. Now, step aside. I have to change my clothes and pack, and please saddle up Strawberry for me."

Waity returned to the house. Sara turned to Chet, "If anything should happen to Waity, I don't know what I would do."

"I understand, but Waity is a determined woman, and from the short time I've known her, I wouldn't want to be on her bad side."

"That's true," agreed Sara. "Especially when it comes to her children, she's like a mama bear."

"Sounds like a deadly combination, Bear Willis and Mama Bear Waity."

Ten minutes later, Waity was back. Chet had to blink twice before recognizing her. Waity had transformed herself from an attractive pioneer wife to a tough, if smaller, version of a no-nonsense gunslinger. She wore a pair of Bear's pants instead of her calico dress. Waity had rolled the legs up and wore a pair of suspenders to keep the pants from falling. She had put on an old canvas coat that fell to her knees and tucked her long brown hair under a slouched wool hat. Waity had stuck a pistol and a large skinning knife into the wide leather belt that encircled her waist. Over her shoulders were two saddlebags and a Harpers Ferry 1841 Rifle.

Little Jedidiah and Rose looked up at their mother with sad eyes. Rose bit her lower lip, trying hard not to cry.

Waity bent down and kissed each child. "Now, you two be good for your Aunt Sara, and don't worry, Pa will be home soon."

The two children nodded their heads.

Waity hugged Sara and, to Chet's surprise, hugged him, "Take care of that leg, Ranger."

"I will Waity and Godspeed."

Waity stepped off the porch, slung her saddle bags over the strawberry roan's rump, and tied them down. Then she slid the rifle into the leather sheath and mounted. Waity blew the children a kiss, nodded to Sara and Chet, then, clicking her tongue, rode off down the trail.

They watched till Waity was out of sight. Then Sara said, "Who wants to make taffy?"

All the children clapped and squealed with delight. "I do, I do," they all yelled at once.

"Very well, but first, I must clean and bandage Mr. Henderson's leg."

8

DON'T POKE THE BEARS

I f the brothers are going to California, they would have to take the Gila Trail," thought Waity as she rode west. "I'm only a couple of hours behind the polecats, so if I don't stop to rest, I stand a good chance of catching them before they reach the mountains.

Waity nudged her horse into a trot. She rode hard for a few miles before noticing her horse was favoring its right front leg.

"Whoa, Strawberry," said Waity.

The horse halted. "Let's see what the problem is."

Waity slid her hand gently down the leg. Then she lifted the leg and examined the hoof.

"Dang, your shoe is loose!"

Waity was on the verge of tears. Here she was, miles from the ranch, with a lame horse. "There's only one thing to *do: return to the ranch and saddle up another horse. In the meantime, Charles is being taken far away from me."*

Waity's heart was heavy as she led her horse back down the trail to home. *"I should have checked Strawberry's shoes before I left. I'll never hear the end of this."*

For what he hoped would be the last time, Bear tightened the bindings on the travois. "We're only a few miles from the ranch, Eric. How are you holding up?"

"I don't know what hurts more, my backside or my broken leg."

Bear chuckled, "Cheer up once we get home; you'll get plenty of mothering to make you forget your aches and pains."

"I sure hope so."

"There, that should do it, " said Bear, standing and working out the kinks in his back. Bear climbed back on his mule, Sally, and said. "Okay, girl, I know you're tired, but we're almost home. I promise I'll give you some fresh straw and an extra portion of oats for carrying me around half of Texas."

As they neared the ranch, Odin came bounding to greet them. To Bear's eyes, everything looked normal. He expected to see Waity standing on the porch and the children rushing to greet him but figured they were all napping. "They had a few rough days, what with the flooding and all. *"Well, at least Waity will cook up a nice supper."*

Finally, Bear and Eric entered through the gate. Sara

walked out the cabin door. Seeing Eric tussled up in a travois, she ran to his side.

"What on earth happened to you?"

"My horse slipped, and I broke my leg."

"We had our share of troubles, too, and now this."

"Sara," asked Bear, "What do you mean? We had our share of troubles."

Sara looked at Bear and then at Eric and started crying. "The Simon brothers broke into the house and took Charles. They said they were taking your son for you killing Brett's boy."

"When did all this happen?"

"Earlier today, Waity lit out of here, hoping to catch them and free Charles. We begged her not to go, but she went anyway."

"Where's Chet?"

"He's laid up. That wound in his leg is festering, so he couldn't go after the Simons."

"And the other children?"

"They're fine. We made some taffy to get their minds off what happened. I'm afraid the poor dears ate too much taffy and are all sleeping it off."

Normally, Bear would have laughed at the children overeating, but not this time.

"I'll get Eric inside, then fix me some food for the trail. I must get Sally in her stall and hitch up another mule."

"But you need your rest, Pa," said Eric.

"I'll rest when I'm dead. Now, let's get you inside."

Bear was back in the saddle an hour later, riding hard after Waity.

"Come on now, Strawberry," urged Waity, "I know it hurts, and you want to stop, but we need to get home before sundown."

Waity was as worn out as her horse. She almost wished she had listened to Sara and Chet and waited for Bear. That's when she saw a familiar figure galloping toward her. Waity stopped and waved her hand. Bear, seeing his wife, waved back.

"Waity, what on earth were you thinking? Going after the Simon brothers half-cocked."

"I didn't go off half-cocked! I had my guns and supplies. I would have caught up with them, but my horse went lame. Besides, if I waited for you and Eric to return from your wanderings, Charles would be in California and lost to us forever!"

"We weren't just wandering around the countryside. Eric had broken his leg. So, I had to make a travois. That's what took so long."

Waity was going to fire back a sharp retort, but instead, she dropped to the ground sobbing. Bear dismounted and rushed to his wife's side. Taking Waity in his arms, he said. "That's all right, Luv. I didn't mean to shout. You did what you thought was best."

"And I'm sorry, too. How is Eric's leg?"

"Oh, he'll be fine."

"Now tell me what happened?"

Waity filled Bear in on the events.

"So they plan on going to California? If'n I was them. I take the Gila trail." said Bear.

"That's what I thought," replied Waity. "I figure I could catch them before they got into the mountains."

"I may still be able to if I leave now. You take Strawberry back to the ranch."

"No," said Waity, "I'm going with you."

"Okay, I remember a Yaqui village only a few miles from here. We can ride double, and when we get to the village, we'll trade Strawberry for one of the Yaqui ponies."

"Okay, I guess that makes sense."

Bear helped Waity climb up on his mule's back, and together they rode to the Indian village as Waity's horse and Odin followed behind."

The village was closer than Waity remembered. The chief, José Santos, was more than happy to trade with Bear, giving him a fine stallion for the mare.

"Chief Santos," said Waity, "You're more than generous, trading a stallion for my poor mare."

"It is the least I can do for all Bear and you have done for my people. I wish my braves were here to help you find your son, but they're on a buffalo hunt."

They rode out of the village just as the sun was setting.

"Should we stop for the night?" asked Waity.

"No, I know you're tired, but we must make up for the lost time. The Gila trail is well-marked, and there's a full moon."

9

WHISKEY JOE

Bear and Waity rode through the night. Each dozed on and off as their horses climbed higher into the mountains. Waity thought the night would never end, but finally, she felt the sun's warmth as it rose in the east.

Bear called a halt by a small stream. Waity, exhausted, slid from her saddle, thankful to have a break. Bear led the animals down to the water for a drink and to fill a kettle to make coffee. Odin lay down and watched as Waity busied herself collecting wood for the fire. Suddenly, Waity saw a piece of red yarn hanging from a bush. She plucked the yarn and held it up.

"Bear! Charles left this piece of wool from my shawl, just like I told him."

"So, he's alright?'

"It would appear so," said Waity smiling.

"From their tracks, I say they're only an hour or two ahead of us."

"Then, let us ride!" said Waity.

"No, we need a break, and most importantly, so do the mule and horse."

"You're right, of course," agreed Waity. "It's just that we're so close I can almost feel him in my arms."

"God willing, he'll be back home soon. But first, we need coffee and something to eat."

They rested for a few hours before taking up the chase. The trail rosed into the foothills. All around them was the damage left by the storm. Trees had been uprooted and tossed like matchsticks across the path, making it necessary to slowly pick their way through the debris. The only consolation was the Simon brothers had the same problem.

Bear and Waity had only covered a few miles. Both were tired physically and mentally. But the thought of their son with those outlaws drove them on.

"Bear, look, another piece of my shawl! They must have camped here."

Bear dismounted and placed a hand on the burnt-out campfire. "Yep, still warm. They couldn't have been gone more than an hour or two."

"We're getting closer," said Waity, "I can feel it! Hopefully, we'll have Charles back before nightfall."

Encouraged, they pushed forward.

As they rode up the mountain, the trail narrowed. Steep

mountainsides bordered both sides of the path. Rounding a corner, Odin started growling, and Bear's mule refused to go forward. "Somethings up!" warned Bear.

The words were barely spoken before a rumbling started high up on the left side of the trail. As Waity and Bear watched, rocks began tumbling down. "Rockside!" shouted Bear, "Turnback!"

They wheeled around and galloped away from the falling rocks. "We're safe here," said Bear, turning to watch. What started as a few loose stones had turned into an avalanche as the whole side of the mountain collapsed. They watched in amazement as the rocks, dirt, and uprooted trees filled the gap between the mountains.

In seconds, the Gila trail was blocked by tons of debris. Waity stared at the boulders blocking the path and began to wail, "Now we'll never rescue Charles!"

She ran to the rockslide and started rolling the stones to the side of the trail. Bear approached his wife and, putting his arms around her, lifted Waity up and carried her away from the rocks.

"It's alright, Luv," Bear whispered, "We'll find a way. We always have."

Waity cried into his shoulder, but then she collected herself and stared into Bear's blue eyes. "It's as if the gods themselves are against us. First, the storm, then Eric breaks his leg, and the Simon brothers take Charles, and now this."

"Aye, Luv, it does seem like we're on a streak of bad luck. But we've been in tough situations before. Let's look at the facts: We know who took Charles. We know they're going to California, and there are only two of them, Brett and Jake."

"You're right," sniffed Waity.

"And don't forget Charles. He's leaving pieces of yarn to show us the way. Plus, our son is smart, brave, and resourceful. It wouldn't surprise me if Charles has already escaped."

"Wouldn't that be something? To see Charles walking down the trail."

"I wouldn't put it past the boy."

"But we still must figure out how to get around this avalanche."

"Yeah, I guess the only way to do that is to go over the mountain."

Waity looked out at the mountains. "That's going to be quite a feat. Too bad we can't turn into mountain goats."

Bear laughed, "Yep, or better yet, a hawk. Then we can fly over the mountains."

As they talked, a man came riding up the trail, wearing an old blue army jacket, buckskin leggings, calf-high black leather boots, and a Mexican sombrero. Behind his horse was a tired-looking donkey carrying a canvas-covered load on its back.

The man stopped a few feet from Waity and Bear. He removed his sombrero and wiped a rag through his snow-white hair. "See Dusty, I'd told you the rail would be blocked."

Then he looked at Waity and Bear, "Greetings strangers, "My name is Whiskey Joe. The name ain't got nothing to do with my drinking. The fact is, I don't drink. Which is why I'm called Whiskey Joe, but you can call me Joe."

"Hello, Joe," replied Bear. "I'm Bear Willis, and this is my wife, Waity."

Joe nodded, "Say, I heard about you. Is that critter staring at me, a big dog or a small horse?

Bear chuckled, "Neither, It's an Irish Wolfhound."

"You don't say. "I'm sure glad the hounds Irish, and not a Scottish Wolfhound?"

"Why's that?'

"Cause I'm Scottish on my mother's side!" laughed Joe.

"So are you folks figuring on staking out a claim here, or are you traveling through?"

Bear smiled, "Well, we were planning on traveling through. But, then, the side of the mountain ended up in the trail."

"That would be a problem," admitted Whiskey Joe.

"Yep, it would," replied Bear.

Waity, growing tired of this bantering, said, "We ain't got time to chit-chat! Our son has been kidnapped by two ruthless outlaws. Do you know of another way around this rockslide?"

Whiskey Joe took off his sombrero. "I'm sorry for your troubles, ma'am. I do know an old Indian trail. It's a mite steep and rocky, but it'll get you to the other side, sure enough."

"Then, if it isn't too much trouble, can you show us?"

"I was planning on going that way myself. Just follow me."

Whiskey Joe turned around and slowly rode back down the Gila Trail with Bear and Waity behind him.

"You were pretty sharp with that man," commented Bear.

"I'll never understand you men." Snapped Waity. "if I left it up to you. We would still be back there jawing."

"And, I'll never understand women." Laughed Bear.

They rode in silence until Whiskey Joe halted. "Well, there she be. I haven't been up there since the storm, so watch your step and don't crowd up, just in case."

"Just in case what?" asked Waity.

"Oh, just in case there's a rattler. The hills are filled with nasty critters. So mind your step."

Whiskey Joe was right; the trail was steep and rocky. They had to dismount and lead their horses most of the time to avoid falling. As for the snakes, Waity soon lost count of how many rattlers they encountered. Whiskey Joe would wallop the snake with an axe handle each time and stuff it in a gunny sack.

"My wife tans the hides, which we sell to a trader who ships the skins to New York City to be made in men's belts. I like the meat. It tastes just like chicken."

That set Bear and Joe off, swapping tales about snakes and which ones were good eating. Waity ignored the men, figuring it would be good for Bear to forget about Charlie for a while.

The trail zig-zagged back and forth across the mountain. Every time Waity thought they must be at the peak, another twist in the path would appear. Finally, the trail leveled off.

"We're almost to the top," said Joe. This is the best spot to camp for the night. There's a small spring to the left between those two rocks and enough browse to keep the animals happy. I'll cook up a couple of rattlesnakes if'n the missus don't mind."

Waity fixed Joe with a cold stare, "I've eaten plenty of snakes in my time. So, I'll fix my own supper."

Bear and Whiskey Joe spent the evening swapping yarns. Waity stared at the stars, wondering if her son Charles was looking at the same stars as she was.

The next day, they crested the mountain and started back down. Fortunately, this trail was not as steep, and by late afternoon, they were back on the Gila Trail.

"Well," said Whiskey Joe, "I'll shake your hand and say good day. I know you're in a hurry, and I like to meander along and enjoy the view."

Bear shook Whiskey's hand, "Thanks for your help, Joe, and if you're ever in the neighborhood, stop by the ranch."

"Thankee, Bear, I just might. Then he tipped his hat to Waity, "Ma'am."

Waity nodded and managed a slight smile, "Thanks, Mr. Joe."

As they rode away, Bear said, "You were a bit short with Joe."

"Yes, I was," admitted Waity, "but I have a lot on my mind."

"Well then, let's get to it!" said Bear as he urged his mule into a trot.

10

TUCSON

I'm beginning to fear we'll never find Charlie."

They had stopped for the night. While gathering firewood, Waity found another red yarn from her shawl. She stared at the little piece of twisted wool a long time before finally putting it along with the rest into a pocket. All during supper, Waity, usually chatty, had spoken little. Finally, as they prepared their bedroll, Bear asked, "What's wrong?"

"What's wrong? I'll tell you what's wrong! Our son is being held captive by outlaws. Eric has a broken leg, and his homestead is nearly destroyed by that damn storm! And you have the nerve to ask me what's wrong!"

"I'm sorry, Luv. You're right. There's plenty to be worried about. But the way I look at it, Eric's young, he'll heal, and he and Sara, with our help, will rebuild. As far as

Charlie goes. I swear, I'll find him and bring him home if it's the last thing I ever do."

"I know you will. It's just that every time I think of our son with those two polecats, I want to scream. I really thought we'd catch them by now."

"I know. So did I. I think our best bet is to catch them in Tucson. I figure we're a day behind them. But they'll have to stop to buy supplies for the rest of the trip to California. If I know those two, they'll hit a few saloons to gamble and drink. That'll be our best bet to rescue Charlie."

"I sure hope your right."

"Don't worry, Luv. In another day or two, we'll have Charlie."

Bear and Waity finally reached Tucson as the sun set on another blistering hot day. Their first stop was a livery stable, where they paid two dollars to board and feed the mule and Waity's horse. Waity asked the man if he had seen two men and a young boy. But the man said no, "You might try Pete's Livery and blacksmith shop across town."

"Thanks. Is the Marshall Thomas still around?"

"Nope, Seth retired last year. His deputy, Randall Colby, is the City Marshall now. Colby is a good man and honest as the day is long."

"Well, thanks again,"

"Good luck to you and the Missus. I hope you find your son."

"We will," replied Bear as they left the stables.

City Marshall Randall Colby was sitting at his desk

when Bear and Waity entered the office. Colby looked at Bear, Waity, and Odin and said, "Well, as I live and breathe, it's Bear Willis and the Missus and, of course, your Wolfhound."

The Marshal stood and walked around his desk. He shook Bear's hand and said, "What brings you folks back to Tucson? You know, folks still talk about you and Kit Carson. Say, how about we go and have a drink."

"This ain't a social call. Two brothers, Brett and Jake Simon, kidnapped our son two days ago. We've tracked them here to Tucson and hoped you've seen them."

Colby tipped back his hat, "Two men came into town a day ago. They had a young boy with them. I like to know who comes into Tucson, so I asked them what their business was."

"One of the men said their names were James and Michael Smith, and they passed through on their way to California. I asked about the boy and was told he had lost his parents in the storm. The two men said they were the boy's uncles. I expressed my condolences to the lad. The boy didn't say anything; he just looked at me with sad eyes. I had no reason to question them further, so I went on my way."

"Are they still in town?" asked Waity.

"Could be we had a lot of folks displaced by the storm. It's hard to keep track of them all."

"Alright, thanks, Marshall. But if you find them, don't let the scoundrels leave Tucson."

"I won't, Bear."

Waity insisted they get a room and freshen up before making the rounds searching for Charlie. The boarding house owner took one look at Odin and said, It'll cost you another five dollars for that beast, and that doesn't include a hot bath."

Bear thought of reaching over the counter and shaking the little man until his teeth fell out, but Waity's hand on his arm stopped him.

Sir," asked Waity, "Have you seen two men and a young boy?"

The manager, thankful that Waity had stopped her giant of a husband from trouncing him, replied, "Last night, two men and a boy came in looking for a room, but all my rooms were taken, so I sent them across the street to Maud's."

Bear and Waity quickly bathed. Then, they headed straight for Maud's.

"Yeah, they were here," said a petite woman. "But some cowboys had just taken my last room. So I sent them down the street to the Pink Lady."

"The Pink Lady! Why, that sounds like a whore house!" gasped Waity.

"That's right, ma'am," said Maude.

"But how could you? They had my son with them!" scolded Waity.

"I know nothing about that. People come in here all the

time. I don't ask them about their business, and I don't tell them mine. For all I knew, the boy was theirs."

Waity stormed out of the boarding house and headed straight for the Pink Lady. She burst through the doors before Bear could stop her. A big-bald-headed Chinese man blocked her way. He shook his head and said in broken English, "Whores backdoor. No, come here."

"I ain't no whore, and if you don't get out of my way, my husband will boot you all the way back to China!"

The bodyguard was about to put a hand on Waity's shoulder when a snarl from the biggest dog he'd ever seen stopped him.

"That's right, smart of you, mister," said Bear. "Because if you hadn't stopped, Odin would have ripped your throat out."

"What's going on out here!" demanded a very fat older woman with dyed red hair and a pink dress.

"Don't mean to bother you, ma'am," said Bear. "We're just looking for our son."

"Is that so? Well, I don't give out any information about my, ah, guests."

"Charles is only twelve years old," snapped Waity. "We were told he came here with two men, Brett Simon and his half-wit brother Jake."

"Oh, those two. A lot of smoke but no fire. If you know what I mean."

The madam started to laugh, but one look from Waity silenced her. "I take it the boy was your son?"

"That's right," hissed Waity. "Where are they?"

"All I know is they paid their bill and said they were going gambling before leaving town."

"So," said Bear, "If I was going gambling, where would I go?"

The Madam laughed, "Mister, a better question would be, where wouldn't you go? There are nearly as many brothels in Tucson as there are gambling halls. But the closest one is the Tumblin' Dice. It's just two buildings down the street."

Unfortunately, no one at the Tumblin' Dice remembered seeing the Simon brothers. They stopped at three more gambling halls before finding someone who remembered seeing the Simon brothers and Charlie.

"Yeah, I remember them. The only reason I do is we aren't supposed to allow children inside. The men made a big stink about it, but the owner, Big Mike, said no. So the boy had to wait outside. Every once in a while, one of the men went out to check on the boy."

"Do you remember what happened to them?"

"Nope, the place got pretty busy. I do recall they were losing big time. But I couldn't tell you when they left or where they went."

Waity and Bear started to leave when the man called them back. "You might want to ask Carlo. He's the fellow with the broom. I think he was talking with your son."

Waity rushed to Carlo, "Excuse me, sir, but your

manager said you talked to a boy last night. He was waiting for two men who were gambling."

"Si, his name was Charlie,"

At the sound of her boy's name, Waity's heart skipped a beat.

"So, he was here. Did he look scared or hurt?" asked Bear.

"A little sad, not frightened or hurt. Just sad. I went to the kitchen and brought the boy some buttermilk and bread. He wolfed it down like he was starving. I started to ask him his name when two men rushed out and pushed me away. The last I saw of the men and the boy, they entered Pete's Livery."

Bear and Waity ran to the livery, nearly knocking over an old lady trying to cross the street.

"Whoa, partner," said Pete, the owner of the livery, when Bear charged into the stable, "As big as you are, you might break something if'n you ran into it."

"Two men and a boy were here last night."

"Do you know where they went?"

"Two men and a boy? Yes, they were here. They had boarded their horses."

"Do you know where they went?"

"One of the men seemed a little slow. He said they were going to Californy. When he said that, the other man, I think they were brothers, cuffed him off the side of his head and told him to shut up. He was mad because they had lost much money playing five-card stud."

"Did you see where they went?"

"No, but they did leave with a drummer. You know, one of those traveling salesman. This guy was peddling some magic tonic that he claimed made you feel like a kid. But I don't know where they went. Probably to California, I guess."

"Thanks for your help," said Bear.

As they walked out of the stable. Bear noticed that Waity was softly crying. "Bear, we're so close. I can almost see Charlie."

"I know Luv. We must return to the boarding house, pack, saddle up, and head for California. If we ride through the night, we should catch up with them tomorrow morning."

11

SO CLOSE, BUT NO CHARLIE

Marshall Colby awaited them when Bear and Waity returned to the boarding house.

"Bear," shouted Marshall Colby, "I just got word that two men broke into Jose Carlo's ranch house and robbed Carlo of two hundred dollars and a pair of silver spurs."

"Did anyone see Charlie?" asked Waity.

"I'm sorry, Ma'am, but a ranch hand said there were just two outlaws."

Waity's heart sank, "What did they do with my son?"

"Don't fret, Luv, we'll find Charlie."

"Where is this ranch?" asked Bear.

"About three miles north of town. My deputy is rounding up a posse. You can join us if you want."

"Give us ten minutes to saddle up," replied Bear.

"Okay, we'll meet you in front of my office."

Bear and Waity ran to the livery. Ten minutes later, they rode up to the marshal's office.

The posse, seeing Waity, began whispering to themselves. One of the men approached Marshall Colby. Bear knew what they were saying: "Marshall, tell your men my wife can ride and shoot better than most. Together, we've fought Indians, pirates, and outlaws. Our son is with these polecats, so my wife goes."

"Okay, Bear, but if anything should happen to her, that's on you."

"I understand Marshall. Just tell your men not to get between Waity and our son."

They rode hard and fast to Jose Carlo's ranch. As they rode, a million thoughts ran through Waity's mind. *"If the Simon brothers didn't have Charlie, where was he, dead? Maybe they got Charlie tied up someplace. Or maybe the ranch hand didn't see him. Or maybe Charlie escaped and is wandering around trying to find his way home."*

Waity clung to the last option: *"Charlie's a clever lad. If he has escaped, he would know what to do."*

Finally, they reach the ranch. Jose Carlo was standing on his porch waiting as the posse rode up. Marshall Colby, Bear, and Waity dismounted and approached the small, well-dressed rancher.

"Don Carlo," said Colby, "This is Bear Willis and his wife Waity. They're here because the men who robbed you also kidnapped their son."

"Dios mío!" exclaimed Carlo, "That is terrible!"

"Senor Carlo, did you see a young boy with the outlaws? Maybe he was holding their horses or hiding in the shadows." Asked Bear.

"No, There were only two men. They broke into my home at supper time, demanding money. When I told them most of my money was in the First Bank of Tucson, one of the men hit me with his pistol." Carlo turned his head. "See the bump. That's where the man struck me."

"Which way did they ride?" asked Marshall Colby.

"West," one of the men, "I think his name was Jake, said they were going to California."

"Can you think of anything else?" asked Colby.

"One man was riding a light brown mare, and the other a grey stallion."

"Okay, thanks, we'll find those polecats and return with the money."

"Good luck," said José Carlo as the posse rode off.

Even though it was dark, a full moon lit the way, making it easy to follow Brett and Jake's horses' tracks. They rode through the night. By daybreak, they were twenty miles west of Tucson and still no sight of the Simon brothers.

"Marshall," said one of the posse members, "Look, two riders up ahead."

Marshall Colby pulled out his brass spyglass. He extended the telescope and peered through the lens. "I can't tell if it's them, but they're riding like the devil's chasing them."

"The way they're punishing those ponies, they'll be walking soon." Said Bear.

"That's just what I was thinking," replied Colby. "All we have to do is stay on the outlaws' trail. Chances are they'll hole up and try to fight it out."

"Can you see Charlie?" asked Waity.

"No, Ma'am."

"Are you sure, Marshall? Maybe he's sitting behind or in front of one of the Simon brothers."

"Well, he could be riding in front, but I don't think so, " said Colby.

"Just the same. Tell your men not to shoot till we're sure Charles is with them."

"You heard the lady. No shooting till I say so." Ordered Colby.

Bear was right. The Simon's horses were played out. As the posse closed in, the brothers rode off the trail and disappeared behind an outcropping of rocks.

"Waity," said Bear, "I didn't see Charlie. He's not with them."

"I know," said Waity, "I didn't see him either."

"Hold up, men," ordered Marshall Colby. "Let's see what they're going to do."

The sound of a rifle shot and a bullet slamming into the dirt told Marshall Colby all he needed to know. "Alright, men, spread out, then move in."

"We need to capture at least one of the brothers alive, Marshall!" yelled Bear.

"Can't make any promises once the lead starts flying, but will try."

As ordered, the five men, plus Marshall Colby, Bear, and Waity, using the cover of trees, bushes, and rocks, moved closer to the brothers. Every now and then, one of them would pop up and shoot. But the poorly aimed bullets fell far short of their targets. The posse crept to within two hundred feet of the brothers. Marshall Colby shouted, "Brett, Jake, this is Marshall Colby. We have you surrounded. Surrender now before anyone gets hurt."

"Go to hell, Marshall!" yelled Brett. "We ain't surrendering and going back to the rat-infested prison. We'd rather die out here as free men."

"Ask them about Charles, " said Waity.

"What did you do with the boy?" asked Colby.

"The boy? Say, is that Bear Willis? I thought I recognized his ugly mug. You tell that big galoot to let us go if he and his pretty wife want to see their son alive."

"That ain't how's it done, Brett, and you know it! Now, this is your last chance. Throw down your guns and walk out with your hands up!"

The brothers started shooting again. Unfortunately, a bullet hit one of Colby's men. The man cried out and fell to the ground. Two men rushed to the wounded man and dragged him to safety.

"How bad is he?" asked Colby.

"It's bad, Marshall. Thomas took one in the lungs."

"Damnation," cursed Colby, "Alright, men, give them hell!" Yelled Colby as he stood and started firing toward the rocks. The rest of the posse joined the Marshall. Then, from behind the rocks, they heard a cry.

"Stop shooting, you killed Brett!"

"Toss out your guns, then come out with your hands touching the sky!" ordered Marshall Colby.

Jake stood up and tossed two pistols and a rifle over the rocks, then raising his hands, he walked out from behind the rocks.

Before Bear could stop her, Waity ran toward Jake. Jake stood frozen with his hands in the air as Waity began hitting him. "Where's my son? Where's Charlie?"

Jake dropped his hands and tried to protect himself from this crazy woman. Waity kept swinging until Bear wrapped his arms around her. "That's enough, Luv. He ain't no good to us dead."

Waity turned in Bear's arms, burying her face into his chest, and began weeping.

Pointing to Jake, Marshall Colby said, "Gag him and tie him to that tree! We'll camp here for the night; maybe this polecat will be ready to talk in the morning."

Bear rolled over and reached out a hand to touch his wife, but Waity wasn't there. Three hours ago, she had cried herself to sleep. They had been through a lot since they first met. But this was the first time that Bear could remember Waity so devastated.

"Waity has always been a fighter." He thought as he pulled on his boots. *"She's not the sort to go all weepy. I guess this has affected her more than I realized."*

Bear chided himself for not being more aware of his wife's emotions. He searched for her by the dying fire, but she wasn't there. Then she heard a whimper and the sound of someone sharpening a knife. Fearing the worst, Bear ran to the tree where Jake was tied.

Waity was sitting on a log a few feet from the outlaw. Bear's large skinning knife was in her hands. Waity smiled as she stroked the curved blade on a wet stone. Jake's eyes were wide with fear as he watched the blade glimmering in the moonlight. Every once in a while, Jake tried to cry out, but the gag reduced his scream to a whimper.

"Waity, what are you doing?"

Waity looked up and smiled. "I couldn't sleep, so I thought I would keep our little friend company."

By now, the whole camp was stirring as the word spread that Waity was going to slice up Jake Simon.

"Waity, I can't let you cut the man!" said Marshall Colby.

"Every minute we delay increases the chances I'll never see Charlie again."

"Ah, let her cut the scoundrel!" said one of the men. The others voiced their support.

"If we do, then we're no better than him!' argued Marshall Colby, "I'll not let this posse turn into a lynch mob!"

Bear put a shoulder on Colby's arm. "Marshall, a word, please."

Bear led Marshall Coby away from the men. "I know my wife, she's pretty upset now, but she would never cut up a defenseless man. What she's trying to do is scare the truth out of Jake Simon."

"Well, she's doing a pretty good job of it," replied Colby.

"Let's let this play out," suggested Bear. "Remove Jake's gag and give him a chance to talk. Without his brother for support, I'm sure he'll talk."

"Okay, but tell your wife to be careful with that pigsticker."

"You know, men. I've changed my mind. I'll remove the gag and give Simon one chance to tell us what's become of the boy. We'll let Waity go at him if he won't talk."

Knowing the Marshall would never allow Waity to crave up the prisoner, the men went along with the ruse.

"Okay, Jake," said Colby, "You have one chance to tell us what happened to the boy."

Marshall Coby removed the gag and untied him. The first thing Jake did was bend over and vomit on the Marshall's boots. The men laughed as Colby swore a blue streak, pulled a handkerchief from his pocket, and wiped away the vomit. Bear went to Jake. "Here, rinse your mouth out."

Jake took the canteen and rinsed his mouth. Then, Bear grabbed Jake's hair and pulled his head back. "You have three seconds to start talking, or my wife will slit your throat! One, Two,"

"No, wait!" cried Jake, "I'll talk!"

Bear let go of Jake's hair. "So talk! Where have you taken my son?"

"Brett sold your boy to a traveling medicine man."

"What!" screamed Waity as she rushed at Jake, waving the knife.

"No, please," pleaded Jake, "I'm telling you the truth. My brother lost a lot of money playing cards with this medicine man. We didn't have enough to cover Brett's I.O.U. So he offered your son to the medicine man. The last I saw of your son, he was sitting next to the medicine man as he rode out of Tucson."

"You sold my son like a farmer would sell a pig?" screamed Waity.

"Please, Ma'am. I liked your boy. I really did. I tried to tell Brett not to do it, but he wouldn't listen."

"This medicine man have a name?" asked Marshall Colby.

"Yeah, let's see, Doctor John. Yep, that was his name. It was painted on the side of his wagon, Doctor John's Traveling Medicine Show."

"I remember the wagon," said one of the posse. "Doctor John set up in front of the Pink Lady until that Chinese fellow ran him off. The doctor was selling some magical elixir that he claimed cured all kinds of diseases."

"Ain't nothing more than snake oil and alcohol," said

another man. "My wife bought a bottle. It cost a whole dollar! She brought it to ease her women's issues. But it didn't do a thing except give her a tummy ache."

Disgusted, Waity walked away from Jake Simon and returned to their bedrolls. Bear found Waity lying on her blanket and staring up at the stars.

"Waity, would you really have cut Jake?"

Waity didn't answer. She just gave Bear a little grin and handed him the knife.

"We'll leave at daybreak. Hopefully, we can catch up with Doctor John."

12

APACHE SHOWDOWN

Marshall Colby approached Bear and Waity as they were breaking camp. "So, you're going after this medicine man?"

"Yep, and if he's mistreated Charles, I'll let Waity carve him into little pieces.

"Ha, that was quite an act you put on last night, Waity."

Waity looked at Colby, "Who said it was an act, Marshall?"

"You mean you would have cut Jake Simon?"

"I didn't have to. The little skunk took one look at the skinning knife and started blabbering like a baby."

"I'd like to go with you, but my authority ends at the town limits."

"But we caught up with Jake well beyond Tucson's border." Said Bear.

"Did we now?" winked Colby. "I'm never sure exactly where the town boundaries end. I suppose I should carry a map."

"Might be useful," agreed Bear. "And don't forget to notify the Rangers about Jake. The brothers are facing charges for killing and wounding a Texas Ranger."

"I'll notify the Rangers when I'm back in my office." Promised Marshall Colby. "One more thing, the Apache Chief Kuruk is on the warpath. So take care."

"We will; goodbye for now," said Bear, extending his hand.

"Goodbye and good luck," replied Colby, shaking Bear's hand.

Colby turned to Waity and, taking off his hat, made a bow. "And to you, fair lady of the sword. I hope you find your son unharmed."

"Waity smiled, "Thank you, Marshall."

Waity and Bear mounted up and, with a quick wave to the other men, trotted away.

The path they were on was finally drying up from the rains. It was easy to follow because Dr. John's wagon was narrower than most wagons.

By mid-day, Waity and Bear had reached a level stretch of the Gila Trail. The sun beat down mercilessly, forcing the couple to dismount and walk.

"If I remember rightly, there's a watering hole a few miles further up the trail."

"I hope you're right," replied Waity. "I don't recall it being this hot the last time we crossed here."

"Well, it's mid-summer. When we crossed with Kit Carson, it was still springtime."

They finally reached the spring, and Bear was tending to his mule and Waity's horse when his wife cried out. "Bear, come here!" Bear ran to his wife's side. "Look, smoke!'"

Bear shaded his eyes with his hands and peered in Waity's direction. It took him a moment, but finally, he said, "Yep, I see the smoke; it must be five miles or so away."

"Do you think it's Dr. John's?" asked Waity.

"I don't know, but we'll soon find out."

It took an hour to reach the source of the smoke. Off the trail, behind a clump of cacti, was the smoldering remnants of Dr. John's wagon. Waity's heart sank as her eyes searched the remains, looking for any sign of Charles. She was about to paw through the wreckage when Bear cried out.

"Bear over here."

Dreading what Waity found, Bear rushed to his wife's side. There, tied to a wagon wheel, was Dr. John. The poor man had been stripped of his clothes and strapped to the wagon wheel. Then, the Apache used his body for target practice. Dr. John's body resembled a pin cushion as more than a dozen arrows pierced him. Before Bear could stop him, Odin approached the body and sniffed around.

"Odin, come here!" commanded Bear. The Irish

Wolfhound turned away from the body and padded back to Bear and Waity.

"Good dog," said Bear, rubbing Odin's head.

Waity turned away from the horrible sight. "Charlie? Bear, where's Charlie?"

Waity began a frantic search for her son. She returned to the burned wagon and poked through the ashes with a long stick. Finding nothing, Waity walked around the attack site, looking for anything that might tell her what became of her son.

Bear freed the tortured body. Because he didn't have a shovel, Bear dug a shallow grave using a frying pan. Then Bear lowered Dr. John's body into the hole and piled rocks on the grave. *"Probably, more than he would do for me."* Thought Bear.

After burying Dr. John, Bear went searching for his wife. He found Waity sitting on a large rock, looking off into the desert.

"Charlie isn't here, Bear." Said Waity. "I don't know if I should be happy or sad."

"If he's not here, it means the Apaches have taken him."

"Poor Charles," wailed Waity, "When will this ordeal be over?"

"It will end when we have him back safely in our arms."

"I would have believed you yesterday, but now I wonder if we'll ever get our son back."

"You can't think like that. As long as Charlie is alive, We will find and rescue him."

"But we don't know the Apache," said Waity." If we were back north, and the Shoshone or even the Comanche had taken Charlie, we might have a chance of the Indians returning them to us. But here in this damn dry and hot place, we don't know these native people, and they don't know us."

"That's true, Luv, but we've always treated the tribes fairly. If I learned one thing in dealing with the Indians, it is that they respect strength, courage, and honesty. We will follow these tracks wherever they may lead, And when we locate the Apaches, we will do what we must to convince them to give us Charlie back."

Waity knew that Bear meant what he said. But even her husband's great strength and courage had its limits.

"I know my husband thinks he's invincible, but sooner or later, he's going to come up against someone or something that he can't wrestle down or submit to his will. And I'm afraid this might be his greatest challenge.

Bear bent down and examined the horses' tracks. "Looks like there's five or six of them. Let's saddle up and see where they go."

They rode silently, praying they would find their son alive and well. The Apache trail led them to the base of a small plateau.

"The trail goes up to the top of the mesa." Said Bear. "Make sure your guns are loaded, and keep Odin close."

Bear was sure that the Apaches already knew they were coming. "There are lots of places that a lookout could be posted. So, keep your eyes straight ahead, and don't make any sudden movements."

As they reached the top of the plateau, Bear was surprised to see green grass and trees. In the distance, there was a small waterfall.

"After traveling through the heat and sand, this looks like an oasis," said Waity.

Bear merely grunted; he was too busy watching for an ambush to take the time to enjoy the scenery. Suddenly, a small band of Apaches came charging toward them. Bear raised his hands to show he was unarmed. The Apaches rode around the couple, shouting their war cries. Finally, they stopped, and one of them approached Bear and Waity.

"I wish I knew their language," whispered Bear to Waity. "But hopefully, they understand sign language."

Making the sign for peace, Bear said, "We come in peace looking for our son."

The Apache stared hard at Bear. Then, his eyes widened in surprise as the warrior saw the huge Irish Wolfhound standing between Waity and Bear. Odin was growling and baring his teeth, but the hound stood still until Bear gave Odin the command to attack. The other warriors also saw Odin and began talking excitedly. Finally, the brave, who was the leader of the band, said, "Dog big,"

Bear was surprised to hear the Apache speak English. Realizing he might have a way of developing a relationship with the Apaches, Bear said, "Yes, Dog big."

"You want trade dog?" asked the Apache.

"What do you have to trade for my dog?" Asked Bear.

"Come, And we will trade."

The Apaches returned to their camp with Waity, Bear, and Odin following.

The Apache's camp was in a small grove of trees beside the waterfall. Several simple wickiups were arranged in a circle. Bear was surprised to see women preparing their meals as several children played.

"This is a good sign. The warriors have their families with them," whispered Bear.

"But where's Charlie?" asked Waity.

"Patience, he's here. I believe the Apache, we'll trade our son for Odin."

"I don't want to lose Odin or Charlie," said Waity.

"Have you forgotten that I have the bone whistle? Once we have Charlie, I blow the whistle, and Odin will come."

"Yeah, I'm sure Odin will, But it will also give the Apaches time to capture us."

"Then be prepared to ride fast," said Bear.

The Apache leader told Bear and Waity to dismount, then led them into the center of the small camp. An Apache woman came out with two deer hides, which she spread on the ground for Watty and Bear to sit on. The warrior spoke to the woman, who nodded; she went into one of the wickiups, emerging a minute later, holding a leather thong. Attached to the other end was Charlie.

Waity was about to cry out and run to her son, but Bear stopped her.

"He's alive, Luv, but we must be careful, or they may kill us all. Let's play this out as long as we can."

Charlie blinked twice as his eyes adjusted to the sunlight. Then he saw his mother and father and smiled. Bear and Waity smiled back. Bear looked closely at his son.

"He doesn't look like he's been abused."

"No, thank God. Except for his dirty face and tangled hair, he looks unhurt." Agreed Waity.

The woman led Charles to the warrior and handed him the leather leash.

"Your son?" He asked, jerking on the leash. Charlie stumbled forward, causing Waity to cry, "Don't treat him like some animal!"

Apache leader smiled, "So, he is your son?"

Yes," said Bear, "He is my son, and we've come to take him home."

Apache smiled. "This is his home now."

Bear didn't want to argue the point, at least not yet. Instead, Bear asked, "What is your name?"

"I am called Kuruk. Which in your language means bear."

Bear smiled, "You and I have the same name. I'm also called Bear.

The Apaches murmured among themselves until Kuruk raised his hand to silence them. " My warriors say you are big like grizzly, but are you as strong?"

Having an idea of what Kuruk was thinking, Bear answered, "Yes, I have been told that I am as strong as a grizzly bear. But what about you, little man, why are you called bear? They should have called you mouse."

Bear could see that it had struck a nerve as Kuruk's smile turned into a frown. One of the other braves, who knew English, translated what Bear said. Soon, the rest of the Apaches, including the women, laughed at Bear's insult.

"Silence!" ordered Kuruk. Then, to Bear, he said, "Maybe you are so big because you are filled with hot air."

Bear smiled broadly, "There is only one way to find out. I challenge you to a wrestling match."

As soon as the other warriors heard the challenge, they started shouting in their native tongue. It was clear to Bear that the other warriors thought a wrestling match would be a good idea. But Kuruk wasn't so sure. Bear could see in his eyes that the chief regretted now insulting him. But to the Apache's credit, he put on a brave face.

"We will wrestle. If I win, I keep the boy and dog. If you win, you keep the boy, but dog stays."

"You got yourself a bet, Kuruk."

Bear decided now would be a good time to put on a show and removed his shirt. The warriors and the women gasped as they gazed up at the giant white man. Bear's heavily muscled body carried the scars of many a battle. The warriors began talking back and forth, and from the way they were gesturing, it was clear that they were placing bets on who would win the fight. As the Apaches bet, Kuruk's face turned red with anger.

"See his face?" smiled Bear. "He's mad his warriors are betting against him."

"Do you think it's wise to make him so mad?"

"I'm hoping that if he's mad, he'll make mistakes when we fight." Bear turned from Waity and walked around the ring, flexing his muscles.

"I'm thinking you enjoy this," said Waity.

"They want a show, so I will give them one."

Charles, who had been watching, smiled but said nothing for fear of being punished. Kuruk handed Charles' leash to a woman and spoke to his warriors. The men quickly formed a circle around their chief and Bear. Bear expected that Kuruk would fight with a knife or hatchet. But the Kuruk was weaponless. Bear removed his knife and handed it to Waity. Then Bear crouched down and spread his arms wide.

"The only chance Kuruk has is his speed. So I'll let him make the first move."

The two fighters circled each other around the ring, each waiting for the right moment to attack. Bear could tell that the Apache was having second thoughts about this fight, but it was too late for him to back down. Suddenly, Kuruk ran straight at Bear. Despite his size, Bear was quick. He stepped aside just in time and stuck out his right leg. The Apache fell to the ground. The warriors who had been shouting encouragement to their leader fell silent.

To his credit, Kuruk quickly bounced back to his feet and waited for Bear's attack. The Apache didn't have to wait long as Bear swung his right arm and swatted the Apache on the side of his head, sending him into the arms of his warriors. The warriors, shouting encouragement, pushed the chief back into the center of the ring. Dazed, Kuruk tried to clear his head. Bear could have finished the fight but instead gave the Apache time to recover. This earned Bear murmurs of approval from the Apache warriors.

A red welt appeared on the left side of Kuruk's face from Bear's slap. Kuruk, stung twice by Bear Willis, decided to move around the ring, waiting for an opening. Soon, Bear, tired of the fight, decided to put on a little show. He turned his back to Kuruk and started flexing his muscles, then he bent down and pushed himself up and into a handstand. The Indians were surprised that a man so big could be so agile. The Bear tucked into a summersault lt before springing back to his feet. Seeing the fight had turned in Bear's favor, the Apaches cheered their approval of this huge, fearless white man.

Bear still had his back to Kuruk, waiting for the attack that was sure to come. He didn't have to wait long. The Apache launched himself onto Bear's back. Kuruk wrapped his arms around Bear's neck in a chokehold. But Bear had anticipated this move. Reaching back, Bear grabbed Kuruk's long hair, yanked him off his back, and threw him back into the arms of warriors. Laughing, the warriors tossed Kuruk back into the ring.

This time, Bear didn't give the Apache time to recover.

He grabbed Kuruk, lifted the Apache over his head, and walked around the ring. The warriors were amazed at this display of strength and waited for Bear to toss their leader back into their arms. But, instead, Bear dropped Kuruk to the ground, rolled over on top of the Apache, and put a stranglehold on him. Kuruk struggled to free himself, but it was no use. Every time Kuruk took a breath, Bear squeezed harder. In a matter of seconds, Kuruk had passed out. Bear stood as the warriors, seeing their leader lying in the dirt, fell silent, fearing Kuruk was dead.

Bear smiled at his son. Then he bent over Kuruk's body and slapped the Apache twice across his face. Kuruk gasped and took a breath. Slowly, he rose to his feet. When he was upright, Bear took a step towards him, which caused Kuruk to take a step back. Kuruk spoke to his tribe. Then Kuruk repeated what he said to Bear.

"You are a mighty warrior and deserve the name Bear. You could have killed me, but you didn't. You are an honorable man. I will give you your son, and you may keep your dog."

"You are a man of your word, Kuruk," replied Bear. "So, I wish to present you with a gift."

Bear went to his saddlebags; opening one, he reached in and removed a necklace of grizzly claws, which he gave to the chief. "I hope the necklace will seal a friendship between us. These claws are from a great grizzly that roamed the mountains far to the north. May the spirit of the grizzly guide you and protect you."

Kuruk took the necklace and held it high so his men could see it. The warriors shouted their approval. "You must stay and feast with us and tell us stories off the north-land you came from."

Then Kuruk handed Bear the leash attached to Charles' neck. Finally free, he rushed into his mother's arms. Both Waity and Charles began crying as Bear wrapped his arms around them. "Charlie, are you alright?

"Yes, Father, the Apache did not harm me."

"Good," we'll have you home soon. But first, we have to stay for the feast."

"Don't let your guard down, Luv. Remember what the Apache did to that medicine man."

"I won't, but the Apaches would see it as an insult if we left now. Better to wait till morning and then leave."

13

THE POSSE

The feast was a simple affair. The Apache had little but what they could gather or hunt.

"Three weeks ago, a band of white men attacked our village at night," explained Kuruk.

"Because we had no way to defend ourselves, we divided into small bands and fled. Each group went in a different direction. When we finally reached safety, only a few of us were left. I was appointed the leader. Since then, the white men have pursued us. Twice, we were forced to fight. Each time, we lost people, including my wife and our son."

"Is that why you attacked the medicine man? Because he had my son?"

"No. We attacked Dr. John because he was evil. Two moons ago, we welcomed the white medicine man into our village. We traded some beads and furs for bottles of his magic medicine. Dr. John told us this magic potion would cure all our illnesses, but he lied. My people began drinking the brew to cure their sickness. Instead of getting better, many got very sick, and some died. Since then, we have been hunting for Dr. John. When we saw his wagon, we attacked and killed him. Then we found your son hiding behind some rocks."

"Thank you for rescuing my son and for treating him well."

"I planned to adopt your son as my own. In time, he would become a chief."

"I'm sure he would have," said Bear. "But now he comes home with us.

"Yes, that's as it should be. A boy needs to be with his natural father and mother."

"Where are the other members of your village?"

"I don't know. We have found several who were killed by the white men. But most are scattered to the winds. They fear the white men will kill them if they settle in one spot for too long. My band plans to go to Mexico. The Yaqui have promised us land to settle in. But I'm afraid we'll never get there. Even now, my scouts tell me the white man is searching for us."

"I am sorry for your troubles," replied Bear. "Not all white men are like Dr. John and the men chasing you."

Kuruk sadly nodded at his head. "I believe what you say is true, Bear. But most of the white men we have met are deceitful. They only want our land. We may be a small group, but we will fight for our freedom."

"Then I'm afraid you will die," said Bear. "The white men are many, and the Indians are few."

"What you say is true. The cost of freedom is high, but it is better to die as a free man than to live as a slave. If you were me, would you do things differently?'

"No, I would fight."

"If more white men were like you, we might be able to live together."

""Sadly, I've seen what happens when the tribes try to live under the white man's rule. It never works out."

"We Apache only want to live as our grandfathers did. But the whites want us to live in houses made of wood, plow the fields, and grow vegetables. The white man is killing off the great herds. Soon, we'll have nothing to feed your families. Then we'll be forced to live where the white man tells us to live and eat beef instead of buffalo. The Apache would rather die."

The following morning, Bear and his family said goodbye to Kuruk. They had traveled only ten miles when, in the distance, they saw a group of men riding towards them.

"You and Charlie wait here. I'm going to ride ahead and see what they want."

"Be careful," warned Waity.

"I will, but just to be safe. Keep your guns ready."

Bear rode slowly towards the men. From the amount of dust billowing behind the riders, Bear figured it was a large group of men. *"This must be the men who are hunting the Apache."*

Bear stopped about a hundred yards from where his wife and boy were waiting. Bear gave no signs of aggression. He waited for the men and their horses to approach. Leading the posse was a tall, lean man with a long handlebar mustache.

The man looked Bear up and down, then stared at Waity and Charles.

"Who are you, and what are you doing out here alone?" questioned the man.

"I'm returning from California with my family."

The man squinted at Bear, "Mister, you are either dumb or just plain lucky to have made it this far without getting yourself and your family kilt."

Bear shrugged his shoulders. "Then I guess I'm just lucky."

Bear extended his hand. My name is Bear Willis, and that's my wife, Waity, and my son, Charlie. I have a ranch outside of El Paso."

"I'm Matt Holmes. Willis? I recall some of the men talking about a big mountain man named Bear Willis. You wouldn't be the one who came over with Kit Carson back in '41'?"

"Yep, that be me."

"I have to warn you. The Apache are on the warpath.

We've been chasing a small band of them for days. We think they're holed up on a small plateau about twenty miles to the west. When we find the bastards, we'll put them down. Every last man, woman, and child.""

"What did the Apaches do?"

"Mostly stealing cattle, but they stand in the way of progress. If we don't kill them, they'll surely kill us."

"That's too bad," replied Bear." In my experience, we can learn much from the native tribes."

"You mean, like how to skin a rabbit or what wild plant is good to eat?" scoffed Holmes. "Hell, man, they're just taking up room better suited for a white man."

Bear knew Holmes was baiting him. *"I ain't going to argue with this polecat."*

"Well, that's your opinion, my friend. So, if you don't mind, we'll be on our way."

Holmes looked at Bear, "You know what, Mr Willis. I do mine. The way you're talking, I'm afraid if we left. You would go warn those damn Apaches. I can't have that, so I'll tell you what, you and your family will ride with us. We'll let you return to El Paso when we finish our hunt."

Bear fixed Holmes with an icy stare, "I'll speak to my wife and see what she says."

"Don't take too long, Willis."

Bear considered pulling his pistol and shooting Holmes, but instead, he turned around and rode back to Waity and Charles.

"What did the men want?" asked Waity.

"They're the ones who attacked the Apache village. They plan to wipe out all the Apaches. They don't trust us, so they want us to ride with them until the posse kills every Indian they can find."

"We can't let them do that! We must warn Kuruk and his people."

"You're right, Luv. We can go along with the posse, and when night falls we can escape and warn the Apache. I just hate to put you and Charlie in danger."

Charlie and I take can care of ourselves," replied Waity. "Who is the leader of the posse?"

"His name is Holmes, Matt Holmes. I've never heard of him, but he has about twenty men with him, so his word is law."

Bear didn't like the idea of putting his family in danger, but what choice did they have? Even if they went with the posse, there's no guarantee they would be safe. Holmes was determined to hunt down Kuruk and his band, and Bear felt duty-bound to stop them.

"*We've been in tough situations before and survived. Waity is an expert shot, and Charles knows how to handle a firearm, as well as most men. Besides, a team of wild horses couldn't stop Waity once her mind was made up.*"

"Okay, so that's our plan. Follow me, and I'll introduce you to Matt Holmes.

Holmes had dismounted and was smoking a cheroot as Waity, Charles, and Bear approached."

"That's one big dog you have there, Willis. Have you ever put him in the dog pit?"

"Nope,"

"That's too bad. A dog that big would be a champion. So this is the little lady and your son?"

Bear's back stiffened, but he replied, "Yes. This is my wife, Waity, and my son, Charlie. Charlie, Waity, this is Mr Matt Holmes. He's a man in charge of hunting down the Indians."

It was all Waity could do not to spit in Holme's face. Instead, she replied, "It's a pleasure to meet you, Mr. Holmes. It'll be nice to have your men around for protection."

"Well, that's what we're here for, Ma'am, keeping the folks like you safe. Are you sure you didn't see the Indians?"

"Can't say that we have." Replied Bear.

"And you ma'am?"

"Waity shook her head, no, "Like my husband said. It's been an uneventful journey. If we had encountered Apaches, I'm sure vultures would be picking our bones by now."

"Holmes grinned, "Very well. But, tomorrow, you'll get your fill of Indians because I plan to attack that renegade Apache, Kuruk, and his band."

Again, Waity wanted to strike out at Holmes. "Well, I guess you must do what you think is right. My son, husband and I just want to go home. So, if you don't mind...,"

"I'm sorry, ma'am. Didn't your husband tell you? You are now under my protection. After we kill the Apaches, I'll gladly escort you back to your ranch."

"Yes," replied Waity, "My husband did mention that you offered to escort us. But that won't be necessary."

"Perhaps your husband didn't understand. I didn't offer. It was an order. Until the Indians are dealt with, you and your family are under my protective custody."

"You can't do that!" snapped Waity. "Under whose authority are you holding us."

Matt Holmes smiled, "Ma'am, we are miles from any town. The Rangers are all up north fighting the Comanches. That makes me the law, and I have twenty men who will back my decision."

Knowing that his wife's temper would get them in hot water, Bear said, "He's right, dear. We're safer with the posse than going it alone."

Waity looked at Bear, then said, "I'm sorry, Mr. Holmes. You know how women are; sometimes, our emotions overrule common sense."

"That's quite alright. If you'd excuse me, I want to cover a few more miles before dark." Holmes touched the brim of his hat, Then turned back to his men. "Back in the saddle, men."

The posse rode toward the mesa and Kuruk's camp. The mesa glowed red in the light from the setting sun as they rode closer.

"We'll camp here for the night and attack the Apaches in

the morning, " said Holmes. The men dismounted and began preparing their camp. Bear and his family set up camp a short distance from Holmes and his posse. Since being forced to join the group, Holmes and his men had left Bear and his family to their own devices.

Bear gathered firewood, and Charles tended the horses and Bear's mule while Waity prepared supper. After their meal, Bear, Waity, and Charles discussed their plan to warn the Apaches.

"They seem to have forgotten us," commented Waity.

"That's the plan," replied Bear. "We act like we're settling in and behaving ourselves, so the posse will let their guard down. That'll make it easier for us to slip away."

"When I was brushing down the horses, I heard some men talking," said Charlie. "There were saying how much the Mexican government was paying a bounty on Indian scalps, men, women, children, it didn't matter as long as the hair was long and black."

"As soon as they're asleep. We'll slip out the back of our tent and head for Kuruk's camp." Said Bear. "The tricky part will be getting word to Kkuruk without getting shot."

That night, Bear was surprised that Holmes didn't put out guards. When he asked about it, the posse leader just laughed and said, "The Indians around here are real super-stitious. The Apaches won't fight at night because they're afraid that if they're killed, they've killed a spirit and are condemned to wander forever in the darkness."

"So you folks got nothing to worry about. However, if you decide to run, I'll hunt you down and kill you."

"I agreed not to cause you any trouble."

"You're a wise man, Willis, I'll give you that."

It wasn't long before the men, exhausted from a long day on the trail, bedded down. Soon, the camp reverberated with the sounds of twenty men snoring,

Bear reached over to touch Waity's shoulder, but his wife was already dressed and ready. However, Charlie slept soundly and jolted awake when Bear touched his arm.

"It's time, son," whispered Bear.

Bear, Waity, and Charlie reached the horses and mule without being spotted. They walked the animals farther away from camp before saddling up. Then, they mounted and rode up toward the mesa.

14

BATTLE OF APACHE MESA

Reaching the mesa, Bear and his family started up the trail to Kuruk's camp. Halfway up, they were stopped by two Apaches, but as soon as the Apaches saw who it was, they waved Bear and his family through.

"I thought I'd seen the last of you," smiled Kuruk."What brings you back here.

"We've come to warn you and your people that a posse of twenty men plan to attack this encampment today."

"Where are they now?"

"They're camped about ten miles to the east," answered Bear.

"Then we must hurry and prepare for the attack," said Kuruk.

Quickly, the warriors gathered to hear Kuruk's orders.

"My brothers, the white man is coming. We have prepared for this moment for a long time, and now it's here."

"Our friend Bear Willis and his family have warned us of this attack. We will make our stand here. Every Apache has pledged never to surrender. If we run, Matt Holmes and his men will run us down like dogs and slaughter us. It's better to stay here and fight like men!"

As he finished his speech, the warriors started shouting their war cries. But Kuruk silenced them. "This is not the time to celebrate. After our victory, tomorrow, there will be time enough to sing our victory songs. Now to your positions!"

"Chief." said Bear, "My wife, my son, and I will fight with you and your warriors."

"Thank you, but you don't need to fight against your own people."

"You're outnumbered two to one, Chief. Besides, these men are not my people. They are outlaws bent on killing every Indian regardless of whether they have committed a crime or not."

"Then, my brother, we welcome you."

"Where would you like us to fight."

"Your wife, you, and son can take a position across from the camp. There is another trail and rocks to hide behind. The posse could go up this trail planning to catch us by surprise."

"Don't worry," said Bear. "They won't get by us."

"Thank you. You, your son, and your wife will be

remembered wherever Apaches gather." They ran across the camp to where two Apaches were waiting. Bear looked down at the trail winding up to the mesa. Using sign language, Bear made the two warriors understand they could roll rocks down on the attackers. The Apaches nodded and gathered rocks to throw down on the attackers.

"Why not just shoot them?" asked Charles.

"We could do that," said Bear, "But we only have so much shot and powder, but we have plenty of rocks. If you do have to shoot, remember what I told you. Pick your target, aim for the chest, take a breath, let it out slowly, and squeeze the trigger."

"Yes, Pa,"

"It's okay to be scared. A brave warrior is always afraid but fights anyway."

Waity quickly hugged his son, "I'm sorry, Charlie, after all you've been through. You're way too young to be killing men. But we're outnumbered and need every able-bodied person to fight."

"I understand, Ma. I will do my best."

"We know you will, son. But, if you don't want to fight at any time, just lay the rifle down."

Charlie looked at his mother, "I will fight. I'm a Willis, and Willis's don't run."

Bear felt a lump in his throat as he looked at his young son. *"Only twelve and already a man. On the frontier, a boy doesn't have a chance to enjoy just being a child."*

Matt Holmes and his men arrived at the mesa's base by midmorning. Holmes gathered his men around him.

"Listen up! As far as we know, there are maybe ten Indians on top of that mountain. Plus, we have to assume Bear Willis and his wife. By all accounts, they are deadly shots. I've been told there are two ways to the top. One is this trail here, and around the other side is a smaller trail. So here's my plan. We will attack the main trail. But, I need volunteers to go up the other trail and hopefully surprise the Apaches."

"Hell, Holmes," said one of the men. "They could pick us off like fish in a barrel."

"I admit they have the advantage," replied Holmes. "But we outnumber the Apaches. Look up at that trail. See, there are plenty of rocks and trees to hide behind. Even a ditch runs from halfway up the path to the top. If we divide our forces and send some men up that trench, we should be able to take the Apaches."

"You know," said another man. "You're paying us five dollars a day to go chase these Indians around Texas, and that was fine. Like every man here, my family has been attacked, and our cattle have been stolen by these Indians. But what you're proposing is suicide, and at five dollars a day, it ain't worth it. I'm going home!"

A few men murmured their agreement. Holmes realized he had to act fast.

"You take one more step towards your horse, and I'll put

a bullet in you and anyone else who's a coward and doesn't want to fight the Apaches.'

"I ain't no coward! But these Indians can't stay up there forever. Sooner or later, they got to come down, and then we'll catch them and string the Apaches up."

"You don't know that!" shouted another man. "They could hold out for a long time. I've got a farm and family to take care of."

"You know how these Apaches are," replied Holmes. "They could sneak down, and we wouldn't even know it until we return to our homes and find your family dead. So, do you really want to go home and tell your wife that you didn't have the backbone to fight the Apaches when we had them cornered?"

"I still don't like the idea."

"Ain't none of us like it." said another man. "But we have to do what we have to do.

"I say it's time to teach these Apaches a lesson." Yelled another man.

Soon, the posse hurled insults at the Apaches as they tried to build their courage.

"Is there anyone else got something to say?" asked Holmes. "If not, I need six volunteers to go up the back trail."

It took a minute, but finally, one man's hand went up. "For God's sake, men, do you want to live forever."

Then another man volunteered, and another and soon six men stood.

"Okay," said Holmes, "Head over there now, and when the shooting starts, climb up. The rest of you make damn sure you got plenty of bullets and take some water. This could be a long fight. And if you see Bear Willis, his wife or kid, don't hesitate, shoot them!"

Bear and Waity peered over the ledge. "There's some men down at the base of the cliff," said Waity. "It looks like they're planning to come up the trail."

"Okay," said Bear, "Let them get about halfway, and then we can start throwing rocks."

Behind him, Bear could hear the sounds of gunfire and yelling.

"It sounds like Kuruk is under attack. "He wanted to rush to the Apache leader's aid, but then Charlie yelled, "Pa, here they come!"

They watched as the attackers slowly wound their way up the side of the mesa.

"Wait!" ordered Bear as he held up his right hand. "Now!"

Charlie, Waity, Bear, and the two Apaches started rolling and throwing rocks at their attackers. One man tried to duck behind a log, but it was too late as a large boulder crashed into him, hurdling the man down the cliff. Another man was hit between the eyes with a small rock thrown by Charlie. He fell backward into the man behind him as the rest of the men dashed for shelter.

"Hold up a moment," said Bear, "Let's see what they're going to do."

As they watched one man, then another cautiously started back up the trail. Bear picked up his long rifle and squeezed the trigger. The fifty-caliber lead shot slammed into the man's chest, throwing him against his other companions. The remaining attackers dove to the ground, trying to burrow into the dirt.

Once again, Bear raised his hand. "That should give them something to think about."

They watched as one man pulled a white handkerchief from his pocket and waved it. Bear cupped his hands around his mouth and yelled, "We won't shoot! Turn back now and go home!"

The remaining attackers turned and quickly stumbled back down the trail.

"They're retreating," said Waity.

"Yep, I don't think they got the stomach for it." Said Bear. "I don't think we'll have any more trouble from them."

Suddenly, a volley of fire and men shouting made Bear look across the camp to where Kuruk and his warriors struggled to push back another attack.

"You and Charlie stay here. Odin, stay!" Then Bear turned to the warriors, who had guarded the back trail with them. Bear pointed and ran across the camp with the two Apaches right behind them.

Kuruk and his men were in danger of being overrun by Holmes's posse. Bear rushed to the edge of the mesa and looked down. Holmes's men were climbing up the trail.

"That's odd." thought Bear.

At the base of the mesa, Bear saw a few men sitting on the ground. They appeared to have their hands tied and were guarded by two men with rifles.

Bear didn't have time to ponder the sight as a man's scream of agony brought him back to the battle. Without hesitating, Bear waded into the fight. Swinging the rifle, Bear knocked one man down. Then he smashed the rifle's stock into the face of another attacker. The force of the blow shattered the man's nose in a spray of blood and mucus.

Bear turned as another of Holmes's men, waving a trade hatchet, rushed at Bear.

Bear raised his rifle in an attempt to block the hatchet. But the hatchet's head caught hold of Bear's rifle, and with a twist, the Long Rifle was torn from his hands.

Bear pulled his knife and slashed at his attacker. This time, the blade dug deep into the man's stomach. Screaming, he dropped his hatchet and fell to his knees as his guts spilled into his hands.

Above the din of battle, Bear heard Kuruk's war cry. The Apache chief was surrounded by men. Kuruk stabbed at the men with his lance. At the Apache's feet were three dead white men, victims of Kuruk's spear.

The Apache chief was bleeding from multiple wounds. Bear could tell the Kuruk was exhausted. *"If I don't help Kuruk, he'll die!"* Thought Bear.

Shouting his own cry, Bear ran to Kuruk's side. Bear grabbed one of the attackers by the back of his shirt and tossed him screaming over the cliff. Another man charged Bear, who stepped aside and tripped him with his leg. Then Bear threw the man back down the path.

Bear looked at Kuruk, "This is not your fight," said Kuruk, "Take your family and go."

"No," shouted Bear, "We made our decision. My family stands with the Apaches!"

Fortunately, the trail up to the top of the mesa was narrow and steep. Limiting the number of men who could fight at any one time.

Still, Kuruk's small band of warriors was gradually being beaten back. Each Apache, who could still fight, had suffered several wounds. Bear marveled at the Apache's bravery.

"They have fought well, but eventually, Holmes and his posse will slaughter them all."

The battle waged back and forth, each side punishing the other, as one by one another, Apache was killed. Matt Holmes, who had been watching the fight from below, sensing victory, climbed up to the top. Seeing Bear, Holmes raised his pistol and fired. The bullet whizzed by Bear's right ear and buried itself in the left shoulder of the man Bear was fighting.

"Holmes, you bastard! You shot me!" screamed the man as he dropped to his knees.

Bear turned to face Holmes, "Damn you, Willis! You and your family will pay for your standing with these heathens!"

Holmes pointed his pistol at Bear and pulled the trigger. But the gun misfired. With a roar, Bear charged. Holmes threw his pistol at Bear. But the revolver merely bounced off the big man's chest as Bear slammed into Holmes, driving the smaller man to the ground. In a rage, Bear landed on Matt Holmes and wrapped his hands around Holmes's neck. His eyes bulged out, and his face went from red to purple as Bear squeezed the life out of the posse leader.

Holmes's hands tore at Bear's arms, but it was useless. In desperation, Holmes searched the ground for anything he could use to knock Bear off him. The dark veil of death descended on him when, in one last effort, Holmes tossed a handful of dirt into Bear's eyes. Bear howled in shock and pain as the dirt stung and blinded him. Bear let go of Holmes and rolled off the outlaw. Then, on all fours, he crept away, hoping to buy himself some time for his tears to wash out the dirt.

Holmes, coughing and wheezing, struggled to his feet. Then, seeing Bear on the ground trying to clear his eyes with his hands, Holmes grunted and began kicking Bear. Bear, still partially blinded, rolled away from his attacker. But Holmes was relentless as he delivered one kick after another into Bear's body.

Holmes brought his leg back, hoping to deliver another kick. But Bear, his vision clearing, grabbed the leg and, pulling hard, dumped Holmes on his back. The outlaw hit the ground hard. Bear crawled over to Holmes and, finding a rock, smashed it into the man's skull, killing him instantly. Bear rolled off the outlaw's body and lay there catching his breath.

The Apaches, emboldened by the death of the posse's leader, managed to drive the attackers back down the trail.

Dimly, Bear saw Kuruk bend down and offer Bear a hand. Bear reached up and grabbed Kuruk's forearm. Bear was astonished at the Apache's strength, who, although wounded, quickly lifted Bear.

All around, Bear and Kuruk lay dead and dying men. "This ends now!" growled Bear.

Bear picked up Holmes' body and walked to the cliff's edge. Bear held up Holmes for all the posse to see. "You men," shouted Bear, "here is your leader. Take his body, and your dead and wounded, and go! The Apaches will not harm you. They only want to join their brothers in Mexico. But be quick before they change their minds."

Then, turning to Kuruk, Bear said, "Chief, go back to your camp and tend to your wounded. I'll stay here and make sure the posse leaves."

Kuruk nodded, then spoke to his warriors. Quickly, the Apache collected the dead and injured and brought them back to the camp. Bear watched as Waity and Charlie helped the Apaches care for their wounded.

Cautiously, the remainder of Holmes's men ventured back onto the mesa. Bear stood silently as the men moved their wounded and dead back down to the mesa's base. One man, a short but muscular redhead, approached Bear and held out his hand. Bear shook the man's hand. "Abe Franks is my name, Mr. Willis. I just wanted you to know that some of us didn't want this to happen. We only wanted to drive the Apache out of Texas. Unfortunately, Holmes and the hotheads were out for blood. Some of the men had lost livestock and saw their families butchered. We tried to stop this killing by holding back and refusing to fight. Holmes swore he'd hang us for not fighting, calling us traitors and cowards."

"That was you who were under guard?"

"Yes," replied Abe.

"It is a brave man, not a coward, who's willing to die rather than obey an unjust order."

"Thank you, Bear."

"Come with me, Abe. I'd like you to meet Chief Kuruk."

As they walked to the circle of huts, Waity and Charlie ran toward them, with Odin bounding alongside them. Charlie sprinted ahead, "Pa," shouted Charlie as he jumped into Bear's arms. "Whoa, Charlie," laughed Bear, setting his son down, "you're a man now."

Bear lowered Charlie to the ground, then his wife wrapped her arms around his neck.

"I thought you were a goner," said Waity.

"Remember, Ma," said Charlie, "Pa can't die!"

"I'm started to believe that," smiled Waity.

Abe nervously cleared his throat, "Oh, Waity, Charles, this is Abe. He and a few other men refused to fight. So Holmes tied them up and threatened to hang them."

"That took a lot of courage, Abe." Said Waity.

"At the time, it seemed the right thing to do."

"I'm taking him to meet Chief Kuruk."

"Good, Charlie and I will be helping the women care for the injured braves."

Later, after the wounded had been treated and the dead prepared for burial, Chief Kuruk and two of his senior warriors sat around a fire with Bear and Abe.

"It is good of you to escort my people to the border." Said Kuruk.

"It's the least we can do," said Abe. "We'll ride under a flag of truce. Also, one of the men has an American flag. So, I doubt we'll have any troubles."

"I want you to know that it wasn't my warriors who've been raiding and killing. We've seen enough death and only wish to live in peace."

"I hope you will find peace in Mexico," replied Abe.

"Who knows, the Yaqui have promised us land high up in the mountains, far away from the Mexican Federales."

Then Chief Kuruk turned to Bear. "Bear Willis, I had heard many stories about the giant mountain man from the north. I did not believe the stories could be true. But after meeting you and seeing you and your family fight. I believe the stories only tell half the truth."

Bear chuckled, "It's hard to live up to the stories, but I try."

"It's been a hard day," said Kuruk, "We've lost good men, brave warriors. Tomorrow, we will bury our dead. This is a private time of mourning, so we ask you to wait for us below. We will join you the day after the burial."

Abe nodded as Bear said, "I understand, Chief Kuruk, and will honor your request."

"Then, I will bid you good night."

The men stood and shook hands.

Bear and Abe returned to where Waity, Charles, and Odin were waiting.

"If you told me that I'd be sitting down talking to an Apache War Chief a few days ago, I'd think you were crazy." Said Abe.

"We live in interesting times," replied Bear. "My heart is sad for the native peoples. I fear their time as a free people is fast disappearing."

"Yes, it is sad, but at the same time, it's exciting to see civilization come to the frontier."

"Hmm, I'm not sure that's a good thing."

15

HOMECOMING DELAYED

When we get to Tucson, we'll first take a long hot bath." Said Waity.

"Ah, Pa, do I have to? I was hoping to have a root beer."

"You heard your Ma, bath first, then root beer."

"I'm so tired of sleeping on the ground and eating beans and bacon," commented Waity. "I can't wait to have a good meal and sleep in a clean bed."

Bear and his family chatted back and forth as they neared Tucson. The last several days had been rough. But now battered and bruised, they were all looking forward to stopping in Tucson for some needed rest.

The closer they got to the town, the more people they encountered going about their daily business. So they weren't suspicious when four men on horseback approached. It wasn't until they were close that Bear recognized one of the men.

"That's Marshall Randall Colby on the bay," said Bear. Bear raised a hand and pulled his mule over to the side of the road.

"They don't look too happy," replied Waity.

"Nope, sometimes, being a lawman is a thankless job."

As the Marshal rode nearer, Bear said, "Morning, Marshall,"

Colby nodded, "Bear, Mrs. Willis, is this your son Charles?"

"Yep," replied Bear.

"I heard you found him," replied Colby.

Bear noticed that the three men with Marshall Colby had positioned themselves around Colby and rested their hands on their guns.

"Yes, thank the Good Lord. We had ourselves quite an adventure, and we're looking forward to a bath and a good meal in your fair town."

"Well, Bear, I'm sorry to have to do this, but I got a warrant for your arrest, signed by Judge Izra Bean."

"What? Is this some kind of a joke? What are the charges?"

"I'm afraid, Bear, that it's no joke. The charges are aiding and abetting a band of Apaches and murdering Matthew Holmes."

"That's crazy," shouted Waity, "Bear was just trying to

prevent bloodshed. It was that fool Holmes that started it by attacking the Apaches!"

"I'm sorry, Ma'am, Bear will get his day in court. But right now, I must carry out the warrant."

"Wait, Marshall. We only came from the battle. How the heck did the judge have time to issue a warrant.?"

"Two of Matt Homes men headed straight from the battle to Judge Bean's home."

Charles pulled out the pistol that Bear had given him. "You ain't arresting my Pa!"

The deputies all went for their guns.

"Whoa!" shouted Bear, "Marshall, tell your men to holster their guns. Charlie, give your Ma that pistol. I'll go with Marshall Colby. I'm sure we can straighten this out quickly and be on our way."

As they rode into Tucson, Bear said, "Randall, what's this all about?"

The Marshall slowed his horse to a walk and waited till his deputies were out of earshot.

"I'm afraid you stepped into a real mess, Bear. Judge Bean has had his eyes on a large parcel of land. This land is claimed by the Apaches. The judge hired Holmes to drive the Apaches off their land or kill them if they refused to go. Everything was going to plan until you showed up."

"But, like Waity said, I was trying to stop the killing. Unfortunately, Holmes didn't want to negotiate. He only wanted to kill the Apaches."

"Did you or did you not kill Matthew Holmes?"

"Only after he attacked me."

"Look, Bear, I believe you. Holmes was nothing more than a hired gun. If it was up to me, I would be pinning a medal on your chest instead of putting you in the slammer." Replied Colby.

"Thanks, Randall."

"One word of advice: get yourself a good lawyer and quick! If Judge Bean has his way, you'll be tried and hung before you can spell Mississippi three times. Fred Carlton is a tough old attorney who has tried many cases. He ain't cheap, but if anyone can win this case, it's Fred.

Bear watched Marshall Colby ride back to his deputies.

"What did Marshall Colby say?"

"It seems we stepped on a few toes when we sided with the Apaches. According to Colby, Judge Bean represents some investors who want the land the Apaches claim as theirs."

"Isn't Bean the one they call Hang 'em High Bean?"

"Yep, and according to Colby, Bean wants a quick trial and hanging."

"What can we do?"

"Stall for time. As soon as we arrive in Tucson, find Attorney Fred Carlton. Then you and Charlie ride like the wind back to the ranch. Hopefully, Eric and Chet Henderson are fit to ride. Tell them what happened and have them high-tail it back here."

"I will, but Bear, I'm afraid. You've cheated death so

many times that maybe your luck is about to run out. This is one time you can't fight your way out of it."

"No worries, Luv. We'll figure something out."

Bear was escorted to the jail by Marshall Colby. Waity gave Bear a quick kiss and a hug, then she, Charlie, and Odin went looking for a lawyer.

"There's his office, Ma," said Charlie, pointing to a wood sign hanging on a post.

"Stay!" commanded Waity to Odin. The Irish Wolfhound whined but obeyed, squatting on its haunches by the door. Waity quickly attempted to brush back her hair and brush off the dirt and trail dust but finally gave up. "He'll have to take us as we are." Waity turned the ornate door knob and walked into the lawyer's office.

A prim, bespectacled middle-aged woman gave Waity and Charlie the once-over and, wrinkling her nose, asked, "May I help you?"

"My husband has just been arrested for murder. We're told that Fred Carlton is the best lawyer around. May we see him?"

"You're right. Attorney Carlton is the best. Unfortunately, he's not around and won't be back for a week."

"Is there someone you'd recommend?" asked Waity.

"There's Melvin Combes, but he's drunk most of the time. The only other lawyer in town is Timonthy Whitehouse. I'm afraid he's just out of law school, but I heard he's a bright lad. His office is above the butcher shop on First Street."

"Thank you for your help," said Waity as she and Charlie left the office.

"Doesn't anyone around here bathe?" scoffed the secretary as she opened a drawer and took out a bottle of cheap cologne.

Odin sniffed the air and whined as Waity and Charles approached the butcher shop. A stairway on the side of the building said, 'Timothy Whitehouse, Esq. Attorney-at-Law.'

"Charlie, here's a nickel, buy Odin a bone."

Waity climbed the rickety stairs and knocked on the bare wooden door. "Come in," said a high-pitched man's voice. The door squeaked on rusty hinges as Waity entered the small office. Attorney Timothy Whitehouse rose from behind a badly scarred wooden desk.

"God, he's young!" thought Waity. As the short, thin man stuck out his hand.

"I'm Timothy Whitehouse, Attorney at Law, and you are?"

If she wasn't so tired, Waity would have busted out laughing.

"I bet he's practiced that greeting in front of a mirror."

"Attorney Whitehouse, my name is Waity Willis, and my husband, Bear, has just been arrested for murder and aided the Apaches."

The lawyer's eyes widened, and he stammered. "Please, Mrs. Willis, have a seat."

The lawyer pulled a handkerchief from his pocket and quickly dusted an old split cane chair.

"The whole town's abuzz about your husband's arrest. Did he really kill Matthew Holmes and help the Apaches?"

"My husband is innocent," snapped Waity. "Holmes attacked Bear, and he had to defend himself. As far as the Apaches go, Bear tried to prevent a battle between Holmes and his posse and Kuruk's warriors. But before we go any further. "How many murder trials have you handled?"

"Well, none, actually," said Whitehouse.

"Have you tried any cases?"

"No, Ma'am, I only received my lawyer's license last month. Since then, I have written up a couple of wills. But I have read a bunch of murder trial manuscripts."

Waity could feel her heart sink. *"Wait till Bear hears that I hired a lawyer with no trial experience!"*

"Mr. Whitehouse, I ain't one for long speeches, so I'm just going to say it. You're my husband's only hope. I may not look it, but I have enough money to cover your expenses."

As she talked. Waity pulled out a leather billfold and, opening it, counted out a hundred dollars. There's more where that came from."

"Thank you, Mrs. Willis. "This is most generous."

"I ain't being generous. I expect results! Put aside everything else and get to work freeing my husband."

"Yes, Ma'am, I will."

"Good," said Waity, "Where do we start?"

Whitehouse returned to his desk and placed a blank sheet of paper on the green felt-covered desk pad. He picked up a pen and said, "Let's begin by telling me your side of the story."

An hour later, Waity left the lawyer's office, convinced she had done everything possible to help Bear, at least from a legal standpoint. She found Charlie sitting on the bottom step, sipping a root beer and watching Odin gnaw on a bone.

"I only gave you a nickel." Said Waity. "Where did you get the money for a bottle of root beer?"

"When I went to the butcher to buy a bone, Mr. Max took one look at Odin and gave me the bone for free. So that left me the nickel."

Waity smiled, "Well, we won't have time for a bath, but at least you got your soda. Now, let's go see your Pa."

Waity filled Bear in on the lawyer. "Whitehouse is young and has never argued a case in court," explained Waity, "But he's eager to make a name for himself."

"Thanks, Luv. I'm sure he'll do a good job. I know you're tired, but the sooner you get home, the better."

"We ain't going home, Bear."

"What, why not?"

"It's three hundred miles to El Paso, then another three hundred back. Good Lord, that's a ten to twelve-day journey. You could be tried, hung, and cold in the ground long before then!"

"If you're not going home, what will you do?"

"Well, first, Charlie and I are getting a room at Mother Mary's boarding house. Then a bath and a decent meal, and after a good night's sleep, I will help our attorney build his defense."

"Bear knew better than to argue with his wife. "Okay, but try to stay out of trouble."

"Oh, I can't promise you that," smiled Waity as she squeezed Bear's hand. "I'll come by later for my good night kiss."

As Waity and Charles were leaving the jail, Marshall Colby stopped her. "Mrs Willis, I promise I'll do everything in my power to see your husband get a fair trial."

"I'm sure you will, Marshall, and you can start by letting him have a bath."

"Sure, I can do that, Ma'am."

"Thank you, Marshall, and one more thing."

"Yes, Ma'am?"

"Don't let anyone poke the bear 'cause you will regret it if you do."

"Ma'am, is that a threat?"

"No, Marshall, that's a promise."

Waity awoke to the sun shining through their window. "Goodness, I haven't overslept in ages! Charlie, get up and get dress. We have a lot to do today!"

An hour later, Waity was pleased to see a freshly washed Bear sitting on his cot, reading the bible.

"Well, that's a first, you, reading the bible."

Bear smiled, "Well, I just want to be ready in case things don't turn out as planned."

"Can't hurt none. Here, I bought some fancy duds to

wear at your trial. I bought the biggest size shirt and pants the store had and a nice black tie. The store clerk said there's a tailor who'll take in the pant waist if needed."

"Thanks, Luv. So, what are you and Charlie going to do today?"

"I'm meeting with Whitehouse to start working on your defense."

"You planning on representing me?"

"Course not. I'm going to be his law clerk. You know, looking up stuff, running errands. That'll let him concentrate on building a case for your innocence."

"Okay, just don't get too fond of clerking. Cause after this, it's back to being a frontierman's wife."

"Don't worry, Luv. There's nothing I'd rather be on God's green earth except maybe the Queen of Sheba."

"The Queen of Sheba! Ha, that'll be the day!" Bear laughed so loud that the deputy had to come in and tell him to be quiet.

"And what about you, Charlie?"

Charlie puffed out his chest, "I got me a job collecting empty soda bottles. For every ten bottles I return. I get a free root beer."

"That's mighty industrious, son. Well, Queenie," grinned Bear, "I guess you better get to work."

16

MISSED TRIAL

Waity knocked twice on Attorney Whitehouse's office door. Not hearing an answer, she walked in.

Waity was greeted by the sight of Timothy Whitehouse sitting on the floor with his head in his hands, and around him were scattered files and papers that someone had dumped out of the file cabinets.

"What happened?"

Whitehouse looked up at her with red-rimmed eyes, "Obviously, someone doesn't want me representing your husband. Here, read this."

Whitehouse handed Waity a piece of paper. "Drop the case. If you don't, you'll be sorry!"

"Do you know who wrote this?" Asked Waity.

"No, but I have a good idea. Oh, and to make matters worse, I got this notice from Judge Izra Bean's office."

"What? The trial starts tomorrow at nine!"

"I'm afraid so."

"Can't you get some kind of delay because of this?" said Waity, sweeping her hand around the office.

"I can try, but probably not. And you know the two men whose names you gave me?"

"Yes, they were at the Battle of the Mesa but refused to fight."

"Yesterday, after you left, I went to interview them and was told they had left town. I'm afraid, Mrs. Willis, that without those men's testimony, your husband's case is all but lost."

Now, it was Waity's turn to sit down on the floor. "I'm sorry, Ma'am. I'll return your money."

"Keep the money. It's not your fault, Mr. Whitehouse."

"You're not firing me?"

"No, keep it as a retainer. You never know when I might need the services of a good lawyer."

"That you, Mrs. Willis. So, what are you going to do now?'

"Oh, I have an idea."

"You have another plan?"

"Yep, us Willis's are pretty ingenious folk. But it's best if you don't know about it. I do have one question. Suppose a person is wanted for murder in Arizona Territory but escapes to Texas. Is there anything Arizona courts can do?"

"Ah, an excellent question. I'm unsure; however, once this mess is cleaned, I can verify it. But I think the answer is no. To my knowledge, Arizona and Texas don't have any extradition agreements."

"See, you're earning your retainer already!"

"Judge Bean has rigged the trial!" stormed Bear, "I doubt it'll last longer than a day. Hell, I could be dancing my last dance in two days!"

"Not if I have anything to say about it."

"What are you thinking? That you and Charlie are going to break me out of jail?"

Waity smiled sweetly, "It's best you don't know. I have a few things to do. Just have your bags packed and be ready to travel!"

Waity left Bear scratching his head. *"What the devil is she up to?"*

Waity's next stop was the livery. Where she paid the owner for keeping their horses and Bear's mule.

Then, Waity called on the general store and bought some needed supplies.

"You going prospecting, Ma'am?"

"Could be," smiled Waity.

"Well, good luck."

"Luck has nothing to do with it." said Waity, "If one has planned well."

"Indeed, Ma'am," replied the clerk.

Waity and Charles gathered their supplies and carried them back to their room.

"Here're the bottles you asked for," said Charlie. "This cost me two root beer sodas."

Waity laughed; "When we get home, I'll brew you a batch."

Waity's last stop was at Attorney Timothy Whitehouse's office.

"Mrs. Willis, I didn't expect to see you till the trial."

"Ah, the trial. Not sure I'll be there."

Whitehouse looked at Waity in astonishment, "You're not coming to your husband's murder trial? Why?"

"As I said earlier, best you didn't know. However, seeing as how you're on retainer. I have a short list of things that need to be done."

"Yes, of course."

Whitehouse took the slip of paper and scanned the list. Then, he reread it.

"Mrs. Willis, this is highly illegal!"

"Illegal? There's nothing illegal on that list. Is there?"

"Well, no. It's just."

Waity interrupted, "We both know that if my husband goes into that courtroom tomorrow, he'll be found guilty. So, if you want the blood of an innocent man on your hands, then just tear up that list and forget I was ever here."

Whitehouse glanced at the list one more time, took a deep breath, and said, "Okay, Mrs. Willis. I'll do it."

"Thank you, Timothy. It's vital that you follow my instructions to the letter. Here's another twenty dollars. If there are more expenses, write to me at the address on the paper."

"Yes, Ma'am."

"And one more thing. Call me Waity. "Waity leaned in and kissed Whitehouse on the cheek, and then she was gone.

Attorney Timothy Whitehouse sat down, *"I swear if I live to be a hundred. I'll never meet a woman like her again."*

"Timing is everything for this plan to work." thought Waity.

She was lying in bed while Charlie played a game of solitaire. In her head, Waity went over the plan again and again. She picked apart every detail until she had it all memorized. Then she looked at the pocket watch she had bought earlier.

"Midnight, okay Charlie, it's time."

They gathered their bags and loaded them on the horses. Waity and Charlie led the animals down the alley to the woods behind the jailhouse. Tying the horses to tree branches, Waity and Charlie led the mule back to the jail. Once at the back wall of the jailhouse, Waity rolled an old oak barrel under the jail cell's window.

"Okay, Charlie, just as we rehearsed. Grab this end of the rope and climb up on the barrel. Tell Pa to tie the rope around the bars. Then tell him to move away from the window and cover himself with the mattress."

"Okay, Ma. I remember."

"Pa," whispered Charlie. Then louder, "Pa, wake up!"

Bear woke with a start, "Charlie?"

"Up here, at the window."

Bear stood on the cot, "What the devil are you two up to?"

"Take this rope and tie it around the bars, then move away from the window and cover yourself with the mattress."

"Are you two crazy?"

"Just do it, Pa, and cover your ears!"

Quickly, Bear did as he was told. Then, grabbing the mattress, he squatted in a far corner of the cell and covered himself with the straw mattress.

During the day, Waity had noticed a large crack running from the bottom of the cell window to the stone foundation. Along the crack were gaps big enough for a soda bottle to fit. Carefully, she handed Charlie the two soda bottles packed with black powder into the cracks.

"Okay, Charlie, come down. Lead the mule away until the rope is taut."

Waity climbed up, struck the match, and lit each fuse. Then she jumped down and ran to the mule. "Pull, Charlie, pull!"

Charlie and Waity pulled at the mule's harness. "One, two, three, duck!"

The explosion was small. Waity had only packed half a bottle of gunpowder in each bottle. Then, she wrapped each bottle in rags to keep the flying glass from cutting them. Her hope was the blast was just enough to loosen the wall. Then, the mule could tear down the rest.

At first, Waity thought she had failed, but then there was a crack, and the window was ripped from the wall, leaving a hole big enough for Bear to climb through. Waity gave the mule a quick kiss.

"You two really are crazy!" exclaimed Bear as he tried to give Waity a hug.

"No time for that now, Luv," said Waity as she cut the rope. "Get on the mule and follow us!"

Charlie, Odin, and Waity ran into the woods with Bear riding the mule behind them.

Attorney Timothy Whitehouse and two friends sat on their horses down the street from the jailhouse, waiting for a signal.

"How will we know when it's time?" Asked one of the men.

"We'll know," replied Whitehouse.

Suddenly, a muffled blast shattered the silent night.

"Was that our signal?"

"Yep," replied Whitehouse. "I'm supposed to count to one hundred, and then we ride through town whooping and yelling."

"What if we are arrested?"

"That's why I'm paying you twenty dollars each," replied

the lawyer. "If they arrest us, we'll say we were celebrating my birthday."

"Okay, let's ride!"

The three men spurred their ponies and, shouting at the top of their lungs, galloped past the jail. A deputy ran out the door and fired at the riders. "Dang, I missed them."

17

BACK AT THE RANCH

H old her steady now," said Bear.

"We got it, Pa, just be quick. It's heavy!"

Eric and Chet held the last beam in place as Bear drove the wooden peg into the hole securing the beam.

"That should do it. Tomorrow, we can start on the roof." Said Bear as he climbed down the ladder.

Since returning home, Bear had worked nonstop with his son and the young Texas Ranger. The storm had wreaked havoc on Eric's barn, requiring the men to build a new one. Fortunately, Eric and his wife Sara's cabin had suffered only minor damage. Sara swept the cabin as Eric's children chased each other around the woodpile.

The men sat in the shade, resting their backs against the

side of the barn. In the distance, Bear saw Waity and Charlie emerge from his house and head in their direction.

"Here comes your Ma, with refreshments."

Waity was carrying a basket, and Charlie a jug and several mugs. "I thought you, men, might be ready for some cornbread and homebrewed root bear."

'That's mighty nice of you, Mrs. Willis," said Chet. "I can't remember the last time I had root beer."

"I made this batch myself," said Charlie, handing the men a mug.

"Charlie's planning on bottling his brew and selling it to stores when he grows up." Commented Waity.

"Good for you, son," said Chet. "That sure beats trading lead with outlaws and Indians."

"Oh, and this letter from our attorney came today." Waity handed Bear the letter and the front page from the Tuscon newspaper.

"Says, here, Marshall Colby chased the outlaws all the way to Juaréz, Mexico," chuckled Bear.

"Yep," replied Waity, reading what the Marshall said about the jailbreak."

Bear continued reading, "The Marshall believes the jailbreak was the work of a professional gang. "

This time, Bear roared with laughter, "Professionals? Ha, I think Charlie, you might consider becoming an outlaw."

"He already is," said Waity, handing Bear a wanted poster.

"Waity Willis and son Charles are wanted for breaking into
the Tucson jail and freeing Bear Willis. Reward: $250.00
Bear Willis is wanted for the killing of Matthew Holmes
and aiding the Apaches at the Battle of Apache Mesa.
Reward $1,000.00"

"I guess we'll stay away from Arizona for a while," said
Bear.

"Our attorney also says he is working to clear us of all
charges." Said Waity.

"And how is he going to do that?" asked Bear.

"Whitehouse is claiming that because there are no
witnesses to the jailbreak. That it could have been anybody.
On the murder charge, Timothy finally tracked down Abe
Franks and two other members of Holmes's posse. They
are willing to swear that you acted in self-defense. Also,
you were trying to negotiate a peaceful agreement with the
Apaches when Holmes attacked Kuruk's band."

"Whitehouse is earning his money," replied Bear.

"Yeah, he is. So, let's send him another hundred dollars."

"Sounds good to me. You know the times are changing.
It used to be that a gun would solve most of your troubles.
But now, a good lawyer is more important than being fast
on the draw."

"Maybe that's a good thing," said Chet.

"I don't know," replied Bear. "Pretty soon, the way
things are settling down, you may find yourself out of a
job."

"I doubt that," chuckled Chet. "That reminds me, I'm leaving tomorrow. If I don't report back in, the Rangers will think I deserted."

"Tell Old Big Foot we appreciate you sticking around and helping us rebuild."

"That sure was one hellacious storm," remarked Chet.

"It sure was," replied Bear, "I hope we never see another one like that again."

Bear finished the last of his drink. "You know something, Charlie, I'm beginning to develop a fondness for root beer."

Everyone laughed, and Waity said, "Back to work, boys. We're having a going away party for Chet. Charlie, will you kill me two chickens? Sara and I will bake a cake. Chet, do you like chocolate or vanilla frosting?"

"Chocolate, please,"

"Then chocolate it is. Now get to work. You're burning daylight!"

Later that evening, after the dishes were done and the children were put to bed, Waity and Bear sat out on the porch.

"Bear," said Waity, "I have wanted to ask you about something, and now is as good a time as any."

"I know you want me to patch the barn roof."

"Yes, but that's not it. It's about Charlie."

"Charlie?"

"Yes, he's been having bad dreams. He'll wake up screaming and covered with sweat."

"Funny, I haven't heard him."

"Ha, when you're sleeping in your own bed, a herd of buffalo couldn't wake you."

"So what's causing his nightmares?"

"Charlie told me he dreams that he's back on the mesa. You and I are dead, and he's out of bullets. Suddenly, Indians are trying to scalp us. Charlie tries to stop the Indians, but he can't move. That's when he wakes up. He doesn't want me to tell you 'cause he thinks you'll laugh."

"You need to talk to him."

"Okay, Luv, where's Charlie now?"

"Down by the barn, catching fireflies for the children."

Bear walked down to the barn, thinking about what he would say.

"I've known men who have nightmares after a battle. Some blame themselves for something they could have done differently, and others feel guilty because they survived and their friends didn't."

Some drink, some use laudanum to forget and stop the pain, and a few swallow a bullet. It's those damn demons that haunt their lives! I just wish Charlie hadn't had to experience killing and seeing men die at such an early age."

Bear stood for a while, watching his children and grandchildren laughing and running back and forth, trying to catch fireflies.

"It's too bad they have to grow up so fast."

Suddenly, a firefly flew by, and Bear gave chase. Soon,

he was laughing like a young boy, forgetting he was Bear Willis, a six-foot-six mountain man.

Finally out of breath, Bear sat down next to Charlie. "I forgot how much fun catching fireflies was."

"But, you didn't catch any, Pa." laughed Charlie.

"I guess I'm getting old and slow," said Bear. "Or maybe catching these little critters is only something a child can do."

"Maybe," said Charlie, wistfully. "Pa, do you want to know something?"

"Sure."

"I don't want to grow up."

"And why not? If I remember, it wasn't so long ago that you told me you couldn't wait to be a man."

"That was before the Battle of Apache Mesa."

Bear sighed, "Son, if there was any way I could have prevented that, I would."

"I know, Pa. It's just, well, I've been having these dreams."

"What kind of dreams?"

"They're horrible. It's like I'm back in the middle of the fighting. I wake up, but I can still see men dying and hear their screams. It's like the dead are haunting me. I think I'm going crazy."

Charlie started crying. Bear put his arm around his son's shoulders, "It's okay, son. What you're experiencing has plagued fighting men since Cain killed Abel."

"But you don't have bad dreams, do you?"

"From time to time, I do."

"So, how do you deal with the nightmares?"

"Well, it helps to have the love of a good woman like your Mom."

"But, I ain't married," sobbed Charlie.

Bear laughed, "No, but you have your family. All of us, your Mom, Eric, Sara, and myself, have seen our share of death and dying. Sadly, we have had to kill, but it was always to save ourselves or our loved ones. I can't make the bad dreams go away. I wish to God that I could. But I can tell you that with time, the dreams will fade. Until then, you can always talk to your Mom and me."

"Thanks, Pa. That means a lot."

"You're welcome, Charlie. Now go and play!"

Bear groaned as he climbed into bed.

"What's the matter, old man? Can't put in a hard day's work without complaining."

"Be careful who you call an old man," said Bear, tickling Waity.

"Stop that," giggled Waity, "You're not the only one who put in a hard day's work."

"It's hard to believe we're grandparents. I never thought I'd live past thirty."

"But you did, and here we are, old and grey. Did you manage to speak with Charlie?"

"I did, but I'm not sure. I helped Charlie. I told him the

nightmares were something everyone, including myself, had occasionally and that Eric, you, and I were always here for him."

"You're a good father, Bear Willis."

"I am, ain't I," said Bear as he reached for Waity.

Waity's giggles and Bear's laughter filled the house. Charlie listened to his parents, then rolling over, the boy had his first good night's sleep since the storm came.

AUTHOR'S NOTE

In my last book, "Texas-Do or Die." I introduced Captain William 'Big Foot' Wallace. Captain Wallace was a real-life Texas Ranger and a legend in his own time. Chet Henderson is the fictional hero of my series, "Chet Henderson – Texas Ranger."

Here's what one reviewer said about "Chet Henderson: Texas Ranger"

"This book was absolutely fantastic. I could not put it down, so I didn't! It's a must-read for excitement and lots of drama, exciting moments, and characters. Lots of action-packed scenes, mysteries solved, sexy moments, and memories! This Author has you turning those pages and making them look like you're in the story!

You can find my books at: Amazon.com: Chet Henderson: Texas Ranger: A Texan Western Adventure Novel (A Chet Henderson Western Adventure Book 1) eBook : Turner, Peter Alan, Wood, Harvey, Ray, Charles: Kindle Store

I hope you enjoyed "Bear Willis: Comes the Storm."
Please consider leaving a review on Amazon @
Amazon.com: Peter Alan Turner: Books, Biography, Blog,
Audiobooks, Kindle

Thanks,
Peter Alan Turner

OTHER BOOKS BY PETER ALAN TURNER

Bear Willis: Mountain Man Series

Chet Henderson: Texas Ranger Series

Willie McGee: Series

Zach Watkins: Mountain Man Series

Remington Ryder: US Marshall Series

I have also been honored to Co-Author several Westerns with some of the top Western Authors.

Bear Rasslin': A Bear Willis - Marshal Shorty Thompson Western Adventure (A Bear Willis: Mountain Man Novel Book 9) - Kindle edition by Turner, Peter Alan, Thompson, Paul L.. Literature & Fiction Kindle eBooks @ Amazon.com.

Jubal Stone: US Marshall – Blood in the Texas Badlands with Casey Nash

Jubal Stone: US Marshall – There Will Be Blood with Casey Nash

Bloody Rendezvous with T.E. *Barret*

Land Grab with Charles Ray

Hell or High Water with Jackie Paxton

Fearless: Twenty-Five True Stories of Fearless Frontier Woman w/Korra Turner

The Great Western: A Mountain Man Adventure Peter Alan
Turner w/Korra Turner

Contact Information:

Webpage: Westerns Books by Peter Alan Turner (western-books.com)

Amazon.com: Peter Alan Turner: Books, Biography, Blog, Audiobooks, Kindle

Facebook: (2) Peter Alan Turner | Facebook

Email: pete@western-books.com

Please listen to my podcast at Dusty Saddle Round-Up. I discuss Old West Lore, history, interviews with Western Authors & little-known facts. We'll also hear from my Cousin Clem out in East Fly Scratch, WY. Dusty Saddle Round-Up is available on Audible, iHeart, Spotify & at Buzzsprout.

Join "Pete's Posse" & receive a Free Western Short Story:

"Riding for the Pony Express"

https://mailchi.mp/a30d5c2df73b/petesposse

Made in the USA
Columbia, SC
20 September 2023